GERHART HAUPTMANN
Lineman Thiel

The translator:
Stanley Radcliffe retired in 1988 as Senior Lecturer
in German at the University of Bristol.

GERHART HAUPTMANN

Lineman Thiel

and other tales

Translated by Stanley Radcliffe

ANGEL BOOKS
London

First published by Angel Books, 3 Kelross Road,
London N5 2QS

Licensed edition by permission of Propyläen Verlag,
Berlin
Copyright by Verlag Ullstein GmbH, Frankfurt/Main-Berlin

Translations and Introduction copyright © Angel Books 1989

British Library Cataloguing in Publication Data

Hauptmann, Gerhart, *1862-1946*
    Lineman Thiel and other tales.
    I. Title
    833'.8

    ISBN 0-946162-27-1
    ISBN 0-946162-28-X Pbk

This book is printed on Permanent Paper conforming
to the British Library recommendations and
to the full American Standard

Typeset in Great Britain by Trintype, Wellingborough, Northants.
Printed and bound by Woolnough Bookbinding,
Irthlingborough, Northants.

Contents

Introduction

The history of German literature in the second half of the nineteenth century is complex. Processes of regeneration and change conflict with forces of conservation and nostalgia: realism challenges romanticism, materialism is in conflict with idealism. As the century moved towards its close the cause of realism finally gained ascendancy with the literature of the Naturalists – a development to no small degree affected by the military victory of the Germans over the French in 1871 and the surge of industrial prosperity that followed it. Compelling realities forced their way into the field of literature.

The German Novelle, after reaching a peak of development in its cultivation by the Poetic Realists in mid-century (particularly by Gottfried Keller, Otto Ludwig and Theodor Storm), had suffered a decline in a preoccupation with aestheticism and exoticism, pre-eminently in the Munich circle associated with Paul Heyse. Considerations of style and form became more important than content, while contemporary social issues were largely ignored, the late work of Storm being an exception to this tendency. The Novelle, which had perpetuated the idealism of Hegelian philosophy, found itself at cross purposes with the growing cultural pessimism of the post-1870 era deriving from

Schopenhauer, with its stress on the challenge to the individual posed by an oppressive reality. Here Gerhart Hauptmann found new directions for the German Novelle.

Gerhart Hauptmann was born in 1862 at his parents' hotel in the small resort of Ober-Salzbrunn in Upper Silesia. At the age of fifteen he was unsuccessfully trying to write verse. In 1878 he became an apprentice on his uncle's farm, but found the work too heavy for his physique, and in October 1880 took up art studies at the Breslau Kunstschule. He was a failure here and the year 1882 finds him at the university of Jena, studying literature and philosophy. He left the following year to go on a Mediterranean cultural cruise. On his return he took up sculpture in Rome. But his true abilities did not seem to lie in the plastic arts: he had already produced several fragmentary literary works; in summer 1880 he had worked on two historical dramas, and he was composing a verse epic as well, the *Hermannslied*, which progressed only a short way to its intended length of 10,000 lines. He was clearly in the grip of the historicism of the age.

In 1885 Hauptmann married Marie ('Mary') Thienemann, the orphan daughter of a rich Dresden merchant, and set up house in Berlin, living in some hardship. Personal contacts were here established with followers of the new Naturalist movement, then occupied more with theory and attacks on the outdated literary world than with creative writing, though Hauptmann was greatly taken by the anthology *Moderne Dichtercharaktere* of 1885, a collection of poetry and essays in which he found many of his own thoughts reflected. 'I felt immediately that this was flesh of my flesh, spirit of my spirit . . . Here was an intellectual and spiritual generation that was essentially the same age as myself,' he writes in his autobiography, finding encouragement to express himself in similar vein.

Fasching (*Carnival*) and *Bahnwärter Thiel* (*Lineman Thiel*) were written in 1887 and *Der Apostel* followed in 1888. His first successful dramas then appeared: *Vor Sonnenaufgang* (*Before Sunrise*) of 1889 marked the début of German Naturalist drama. A succession of dramatic and prose writings led to the award of the Nobel Prize for Literature in 1912. A number of his works were made into films in the 1920s, while the flow of new writing continued unabated, no longer in the Naturalist mode, dealing essentially with the individual's struggle against intolerance and inhumanity. Courted and then dropped by the Nazis, Hauptmann led an isolated existence in the 1930s. He died at the age of eighty-three in 1946 at Agnetendorf, Silesia.

'Faithful presentation of life to the strict exclusion of the romantic element' was the demand made upon German writing by the Naturalist pioneer M.G. Conrad, launching his periodical *Die Gesellschaft* ('Society') in Munich on 1 January 1885. The industrial expansion of Germany and the suffering humanity it produced gave painters like H. Makart, Mackensen and Max Liebermann their themes, Liebermann being dubbed 'the apostle of the ugly'. In his Berlin home Hauptmann met a number of these painters.

The main impact of the Naturalist movement in

Germany was registered in the theatre. But before the first performance of *Vor Sonnenaufgang* at the Freie Bühne in Berlin in 1889, Hauptmann had already given literary expression to the theoretical pronouncements of the campaigners for a Naturalist literature in Germany, under the influence, particularly, of the French, Scandinavian and Russian realistic traditions (Flaubert, Zola, the Goncourts, Ibsen, Tolstoy, Dostoyevsky and Turgenev). The young Hauptmann, then living in the village of Erkner near Berlin, frequently met and conversed with the propagators of the new literary creed. After writing *Fasching* and *Bahnwärter Thiel* he became a member of the Naturalist literary club *Durch* in Berlin, reading out to them the manuscript of *Thiel* when he joined in May 1887.

Hauptmann was concerned to draw upon real life, and he places the events of both his first tales in a locality he knew well from having lived there for several years – the heath and forest region to the south-east of Berlin and around Erkner itself. He even uses the actual names of towns and villages of the area. The Naturalist writer was traditionally never without his note-book, for the recording of 'actual' experiences: Hauptmann bases *Carnival* on a recent event reported in the local press in February 1887. He keeps closely to the main facts of the case: a young boat-builder, supremely self-confident, brushing aside the warnings of friends as he sets out with wife and child across the iced surface of the nearby Flakensee with his sleigh, and the subsequent events of the tale.

The factual opening of *Carnival* proceeds in flat narrative style, promising some kind of *Kalendergeschichte* – one of those moralising little stories that were printed in local calendars and almanachs for the edification of simple folk. But the story grows into something much more than this. Tension is created by the use of foreshadowing, which builds up with references to pigs that are to be slaughtered, jests about drowning in the lake, the 'death-mask' worn by Kielblock at the fancy-dress evening, a suggested pact with Death itself, and the mysterious warnings emanating from Nature, to reach a crescendo in the closing pages as the terror reveals itself in stark reality. In a manner anticipating his dramatic practice, Hauptmann spends considerable time motivating his crisis before allowing it to explode, as it were, in the last act. The tradition of the Novelle is nevertheless also followed: for here, surely, we have a 'most exceptional event that actually happened' in Goethe's famous definition. And if we seek a turning-point in the action, preparing the way for the catastrophe, it must surely be Kielblock's decision to go out on the ice with the sledge, seeking to wring the last ounce of pleasure out of a festive day.

All this takes place against a Naturalistic background. We meet with ordinary people engaged in day-to-day routine of work and play, experiencing life at a fairly primitive level. The earthiness of their enjoyment and of their work is stressed, and they express themselves in the dialect of their region – another literary frontier crossed by the Naturalists. Hauptmann was presently to write his drama of the Silesian weavers, *Die Weber* (1892), entirely in dialect.

Psychological analysis is acute also. Kielblock's zest for life, his fear of growing old and less able, his seeking to live life to the hilt, are entirely credible; Hauptmann knew his fellow-men well, and how to present revealing gestures and speech. This analysis of the 'common man' is one more aspect of Naturalism in the work, to which might be added the concern with alcoholism as a social problem, which Hauptmann was to explore so thoroughly in *Before Sunrise*. A further technique of Naturalism used by Hauptmann in this story is *Sekundenstil*, the second-by-second account of the progression of an action as though recorded in slow-motion, and a striking example of this is to be found in the closing sequence of the tale.

Hauptmann was not just a Naturalist, however: he was presently to move towards more traditional ways of writing. This direction can already be seen in *Carnival*, in the demonstration of the power of unknown forces to invade the realm of man and dictate his fate. Kielblock is a latter-day Oedipus, behaving in the belief that he is master of his destiny, while all the time a hidden power directs his fate. Symbols of this ineluctable power are contained in the world of Nature, an element that obeys its own laws and has no reference to human needs. The moon shines or is obscured. Nature's appealing surface can conceal a multitude of dire threats – an idea suggested by Hauptmann in his reference to the lake as a cage of ravening beasts, roaring with hunger and rage. Hauptmann underlines the varying moods of Nature in the use that he makes of light and dark, and of colours, contours and sounds. The ice-bound lake even speaks a language of its own, which young Gustav seeks to imitate – another of the instances of foreshadowing in the tale.

So close to actual events was Hauptmann's story, and so specific to its locality (constituting in this sense a specimen of *Heimatkunst*, or regional literature, then entering into vogue), that he seems to have experienced the need to publish it in a place where the connection would not be obvious. *Carnival* accordingly appeared in the obscure periodical *Siegfried*, published in the little town of Beerfelden in Hessen.

Hauptmann's first published work was forgotten until it was rediscovered in 1922, to be included in his complete works for the first time in the Fischer Verlag edition of 1935.

Lineman Thiel did not suffer the same fate of disappearance shortly after its origination, and did, in fact, emerge as one of the representative texts of German Naturalism, overshadowed though it to some extent was by Hauptmann's dramatic achievement. On first publication the work was immediately greeted with enthusiasm by the critics, and it has never ceased to be admired since.

Hauptmann draws here on no known incident; but the events of his tale represent the collected impressions that he gathered from long conversations with a railway lineman in the vicinity of Erkner, conversations which were an expression of his sympathy with humble folk and their problems. It was the so-called 'social question' which had been the prime cause of Hauptmann's espousal of Naturalism: it constitutes a principal element in *Lineman Thiel*.

The classical tradition of the 'hero', for some time already on the wane, here gives way completely to the figure of the 'anti-hero', a pathetically helpless being, who suffers the impact of events instead of creating them through positive action. Thiel is the creature of his birth and environment. Born into a humble station in life, he finds work and relaxation in the severely restricted confines of his local world, and his mind is shaped accordingly. His second wife, Lena, is similarly conditioned: at times she seems little more than a machine – as Hauptmann suggests in the passage in which she digs the potato patch by the track. Condemned by circumstance to live and feel at this level, stumbling as it were through a bewildering world, these beings are little more than instinctive creatures, and hardly accountable for their actions. So inarticulate are they that their actions and gestures often speak more than their words, and receive appropriate emphasis from Hauptmann: the same is true of his early dramas, whose detailed stage directions give an epic quality to them. For such figures, the question of guilt hardly arises. The call is for us to understand: and to understand is to forgive. Hauptmann invites us to understand equally the situation of both Thiel and Lena. The final lines of the tale are full of pity, not condemnation.

Other traditional themes of Naturalism are also to be found here. That of hereditary influence is one. Tobias, the child of a physically weak and sickly mother who dies at his birth, cannot hope to be fit and strong. His younger half-brother, child of a strapping, buxom mother, bursts with rude health. A growing interest in sexuality also makes itself manifest, anticipating the theories soon to be expounded by Sigmund Freud (1856-1939). Thiel's submission to his wife is based not on physical inferiority – Thiel is a strong man – but on her ability to dominate him through her sheer sensuality. His sexual submission to her, indeed, is one of the factors that lead to his final breakdown, for it renders him incapable of open defiance. Hauptmann's detailed observation of mental states is in the best traditions of Naturalist reporting, and constitutes an almost clinical study of psychological breakdown under unbearable stresses. The use of interior monologue (*innere Rede*) is another respect in which literature anticipated the researches of Freud. We follow closely the workings of Thiel's mind on a number of occasions, most powerfully through the use of *Sekundenstil*. The approach of the express train as Thiel stands by the track, or the scene after Tobias's accident, show most effective use of this technique: we witness the registering of each separate instant by Thiel's brain in a seemingly uncoordinated sequence. John Osborne has written of *Sekundenstil* that it 'deprives us of the possibility of a panoramic view; it expresses, though it does not state explicitly, a sense of loss and anxiety in a fragmented world.'*

Yet for all its Naturalistic qualities, *Lineman Thiel* is a work with many other dimensions. Above all, critics have commented on the symbolism contained in the story, much of it applied to the evocation of Thiel's state of mind. Images of nets and wires abound, creating a sense of man's being enmeshed in a process he can neither control nor comprehend. Other groups of imagery centre around the themes of redness and blood, or death and decay. Even the image of the train itself serves as a token of Thiel's pent-up passion, bursting headlong into furious activity. The world of Nature is once again seen to take little heed of human anguish and suffering, as it follows its own independent pattern of being, now benign, now hostile. A contrast is also

* *The Naturalist Drama in Germany*, Manchester, 1971, p. 47.

established between the vital world of Nature and the machine-like regulation of human life in the wake of the industrial revolution – represented here primarily through the dominant symbol of the railway. Naturalism's attitude to the mechanisation of society was one of growing apprehension, anticipating the out-and-out rejection of this process by Expressionism in the early decades of the twentieth century. We often note in Hauptmann's story the mechanical way in which Thiel carries out his regular activities, at times almost as though he has no will.

Hauptmann, a native of Silesia, seems to have inherited some of the mysticism traditionally associated with that region. It appears in much of his writing, and is here embodied in Thiel's devotion to his first wife, Minna. After her early death he turns his railway hut into a kind of chapel where he perpetuates her memory and sings hymns to her departed soul. The little hut constitutes a sacred place (the *Salvaterra* of other Hauptmann works) where Thiel can escape the ugliness and pressures of the world without. Lena's visit to the hut thus becomes an act of desecration. Hauptmann was not just a Naturalist writer; he even rejected pure Naturalism at times, and it is as though two sides of his own nature are played off against each other here. Thiel's own relationship with this spiritual world is as binding as that to material reality, and the clash between the two goes right through his soul: coordination of the two becomes increasingly an impossibility and madness ensues.

Hauptmann impresses too by his gift for conveying the changing moods of Nature. The sensitivity of his observation is that of the Impressionist painter, recording on his canvas the play of light upon a landscape, or subtle tones of colour. But always with Hauptmann there is a symbolic purpose as well, which relates the natural scene to the human events that are being enacted, perhaps nowhere more tellingly than in the moments after the train accident when the sun's setting is presented in visions of fading hope and decay.

The structure of the tale is simple and developments are related in straightforward sequence. There is a basic division into three parts, though no chapters are introduced. The events are to be seen as a continuum, developing to a crisis. Considered as a Novelle (Hauptmann designates it a *'novellistische Studie'* – a Novelle-type study), it satisfies the basic requirements of the genre: an extraordinary event that could nevertheless have actually happened; a turning-point, when Thiel unexpectedly returns home to collect his forgotten sandwiches; and a great economy of narration which concentrates meticulously on the central theme of Thiel's relationship with his young son, Tobias. Appropriately, the story never wanders far from that fateful railway-track: we hear of it on the very first page, and it is here, too, that the story ends. If we look for a symbolic figure that encapsulates the essence of the tale, then this railway track is surely it.

The Apostle is the third 'Novelle-type study' written by Hauptmann during the period 1887-90. In contrast to *Carnival* and *Lineman Thiel* the presentation of Nature is positive: it is on the freshness, attractive quality and invigorating power of Nature that Hauptmann dwells, rather than on its violent, destructive and imponderable

17

aspects. Contrasted with Nature's openness and organic beauty is the supposed wretchedness of man, constricted by the modern state and materialistic values. Hauptmann has embodied a variety of elements here, both personal and social.

The figure of the 'Apostle' himself is based on a real-life experience, which prompted Hauptmann to draw also on other concerns running through his creative consciousness – a procedure representative of much of his literary composition. Many of these interests extend back over a considerable period of time and are often not easy to substantiate precisely. In April 1888 Hauptmann went to visit his brother Carl, then living in Zurich, for a number of months and it was here that he came across the figure of Johannes Guttzeit, a former soldier in the Prussian army, who had turned himself into a self-appointed missionary and apostle of Nature. He was furious when Hauptmann's story appeared, accusing him of character-assassination, but Hauptmann replied that the meeting with him in April 1888 had merely served to crystallise various ideas in his mind. 'Certain events in Zurich were at best stimuli for me. To portray you, I knew you far too little. In any case I never experience in my life the desire to create so-called 'photographic' images. One out of many possibilities is built up by its own creative impetus.'*

More individualised aspects of the Apostle derive from another encounter of Hauptmann's in Zurich, namely with the eccentric painter Karl Wilhelm Dieffenbach (referred to in the story itself as a seminal influence on

* *Sämtliche Werke*, Propyläen Verlag, Berlin, 1963, vol. 7, pp. 1072-3.

the Apostle). In Hauptmann's later autobiographical *Abenteuer meiner Jugend* (*Adventures of my Youth*, 1937) he recollects the encounter with one of Dieffenbach's 'disciples' on the quayside promenade at Zurich: 'Here there appeared in a hair-shirt, sandals on his feet and reddish hair flowing about his shoulders, a kind of apostle. Jesus could have looked like this. Halo-like, a length of string wound around his otherwise uncovered head ... He spoke against luxury, he commended simplicity, called for a return to Nature. Our way of living must cast off what was against Nature and thus antagonistic to the divine'. (Chapter 41.) His actual message is remembered by Hauptmann: ' "Away," he said, "with the eating of carcases! Man is a fruit-eater!" ... Naturally he also condemned alcohol. Similarly coffee and tea were placed beyond the pale. "Let your drink be clear spring water! If you do not wish to believe the man who brings you this message of salvation, then just ask any animal, and it will instruct you convincingly!" '

The age in which Hauptmann composed *The Apostle* was one in which many cranks and valetudinarians made their appearance, some deriving their motivation from the back-to-nature, anti-city yearning of the industrial worker and urban dweller that found a healthy outlet, preeminently in Germany, in the incipient youth movement and the creation of nature reserves, but also deriving from the writings of men like Nietzsche who, for different reasons, also rejected the conformist and philistine attitudes of the times. Some circles were marked by the mania for physical fitness, in readiness for any kind of physical challenge – including that of military action.

Hauptmann was certainly concerned at this time to distinguish between genuine conviction, charlatanism and sheer insanity. He speaks in *Adventures of my Youth* (chapters 39–41) of the crusading efforts of the Salvation Army, but questions the validity of their 'conversions', carried out in a state of spiritual intoxication. He also deeply distrusted Nietzsche in his rejection of a 'passive' Wagner and invocation of the 'Superman' concept, establishing dangerous new patterns of inspired leadership.

Hauptmann reinforced his interest in religious-hallucinatory states by investigating their clinical circumstances (in best Naturalist tradition) at the cantonal nerve-clinic of Burghölzli in Zurich, where he was instructed in their psychiatric aspects by the director, Auguste Forel, an anti-alcoholic. Hauptmann was in any case deeply interested in religious problems and had been so ever since childhood. He was fascinated by the figure of Christ and wrote, or planned, a succession of essays, stories and dramas about him for almost the whole of his life. Between 1885 and 1887 he published a series of *Jesus-Studies* and worked at a drama on Jesus. *The Apostle* is an amalgam of all these forces.

Hauptmann's conclusion is open-ended: he neither brands his figure as a charlatan nor celebrates him as a saint. We must accept him as he is, a phenomenon of his time, with all his strengths and weaknesses. The Naturalist writer's task was, after all, not to sit in judgment. The theme of charlatanism nevertheless continued to interest Hauptmann, and several subsequent works (dramas and prose) deal with it, perhaps none so explicitly as the novel of 1910 *Der Narr in Christo* [*The Fool in Christ*], *Emanuel Quint*, in which a clergyman, Emanuel Quint, from a simple Silesian parish fanatically identifies himself with Christ, tries to carry his mission into Breslau itself, but is rejected and suffers a lonely death in the Alps.

Of equal importance for Hauptmann was his encounter with the works of Georg Büchner, the forgotten dramatist of the early nineteenth century, whose grave he visited in Zurich in 1888. In his Novelle *Lenz* (1836), read by Hauptmann in 1887, Büchner had given an account of the hallucinatory madness that seized the writer J.M.R. Lenz in 1778, and much of the form and procedures of Hauptmann's *Apostle* follows a similar pattern to Büchner's work.

The formal aspects of the work are possibly its most striking feature, and here Hauptmann is clearly indebted to Büchner. Büchner's *Lenz* is similarly an account of a man tormented with self-doubt over his efficacy as an agent of God, seeking God in Nature and through ministry to his fellows, and is left by his author in a state of final utter derangement. The accounts of both authors are essentially lyrical in character, and the presentation is a series of brief snatches of impression, often with incomplete sentences and much use of parenthesis. There is a parallelism of states of Nature and states of the mind, and similar resort is made to the metaphor of light. Even the same word-complexes are to be found, in particular the motifs of anxiety, tears and self-scrutiny. And a certain dramatic quality is infused into the work of both authors through the use of *erlebte Rede* (the intrusion of the character's own thoughts into the authorial narration), heightening the tension between conviction and doubt, between clear vision and hallucination.

The account presented by Büchner's *Lenz* is however more dispassionate and somewhat reminiscent of a diary, and the author gradually draws back from identification with his character. In Hauptmann's story we are constantly in the presence of the Apostle, experiencing his emotional and mental states right through to the crescendo with which the work concludes. Here is no 'Novelle-type study', but rather a symphonic development of themes, recurring motifs which build up to a grand finale, the ecstasy of the Apostle. His worship of Nature, rejection of modern civilisation, longing for spirituality and seeking to convert swell and diminish as his physical energies ebb and flow. The time constraints are strict here (a matter of a few hours) and the space in which he moves is limited, yet there is a constant sense of limits being transcended and boundaries crossed.

In the more lyrical passages of *The Apostle*, where Hauptmann elicits the colours and texture of the natural scene, speaks of the vibrant quality of the light, attends to intensities of sound and movement, he is close to the techniques of the Impressionist painter. His own early training as an artist and his personal contacts with German Impressionists such as Lovis Corinth and Max Klinger doubtless gave added impetus to his adoption of such procedures, which we have already encountered in *Lineman Thiel*.

The story-line, if one can speak in such terms here, consists in flashes of revelation from his past: childhood, military service, proselytising visit to Italy, journey through the St Gotthard tunnel and plans to travel onwards into Germany with his 'message'. In contrapuntal relationship to this strand runs the factual account of his present local progress through the village.

Hauptmann's work was rapidly written, in the midst of composition of the major dramas *Das Friedensfest* (1890), *Einsame Menschen* (1891) and *Die Weber* (1892) and numerous other works, and it appeared in July 1890 in the periodical *Moderne Dichtung* and subsequently in book form with *Bahnwärter Thiel* in 1892. The easy charge that it is merely an attack on charlatanism was vigorously refuted by Hauptmann himself when it was made by Johannes Guttzeit: 'It is poor taste when you christen my Apostle a charlatan, hypocrite, confidence trickster, etc. To characterise something in a few words is difficult. With more time and calm, you would have found a more telling formulation. You certainly do not seem to be a penetrating psychologist – you jump to snap conclusions. There is something petty about this feeling a personal reference. Why do people find it so difficult to escape from their own ego?'

This selection of Hauptmann's early prose work constitutes a seminal fount of interests and themes that run as a fluctuating stream throughout the rest of his oeuvre. The social compassion and the concern for humane values that speaks in all these three early works continues to be sounded, and it is the style and manner that change, rather than the message. The theme of an inadequate humanity in contest with the powers of Fate (represented by Kielblock and Thiel) belongs par excellence to the realm of drama, and it is to this genre that Hauptmann transferred it with his first Naturalist plays, again presenting mostly the lower levels of society. Elements of his concern with charlatanism also manifest themselves here. The more epic (even lyric) concern with spiritual experience and doubts over the legitimacy of the man of vision which is the main burden of *The Apostle* finds continuing echoes in the prose works of all the succeeding years. There is a movement, too, in the direction of religious mysticism, already foreshadowed in the relationship of Thiel to his first wife, Minna. Hauptmann's is a substantial and many-faceted achievement.

Carnival

Sail-maker Kielblock had been married for a year. He possessed a fine little property by the lake, a house, a farmyard, garden and some land. In the stable stood a cow, and cackling hens and gabbling geese bustled about the farmyard. In the pigsty were three fat pigs, which were due to be slaughtered in the course of the year.

Kielblock was older than his wife, but for all that no less fond of life than she was. Both of them were just as attracted by the dance-floor after their marriage as before it, and Kielblcok would say, 'Only fools start out on marriage as though it was a monastery.' He usually added, 'Isn't that so, Marie, dear', embracing his chubby wife with his robust arms and hugging her. 'For us, the fun of life is only just beginning now.'

And indeed, apart from six short weeks, the first year of marriage had been like one unending holiday for the pair. And those six weeks had caused very little change in their mode of life. The little bundle of noise they brought forth was left in the grandmother's care, and off they went in a flash, whenever the wind bore the tune of a waltz in their direction and carried its jingle through the windows of their lone-standing house.

The Kielblocks attended not only every dance of their own village, but were seldom missing from those of the surrounding villages too. If, as often happened, the grandmother had to stay in bed, then 'the little brat' was also taken along. A makeshift bed was made up for him in the dance-hall, usually on two chairs over whose arm-rests aprons and shawls were draped as a protection against the light. And indeed, the poor little mite slept, bedded in this way, amid the deafening noise of the brass and clarinets, amid the scraping, stamping and shouting of the waltzers, surrounded by an atmosphere of beer and spirit fumes, dust and cigar-smoke – often the whole night through.

If those present were amazed by this, the sail-maker always had the same explanation ready: 'He happens to be the son of Papa and Mama Kielblock, don't you see?' If little Gustav began to cry, his mother would rush to him as soon as she had finished the dance that had begun, gather him up and disappear with him into the cold entrance-hall. Here, sitting on the steps or wherever else she found room, she would offer the child her breast, hot and heaving from the drinking and dancing, and he would suck it greedily dry. When he was full, a mood of remarkable cheerfulness usually came over him, which gave his parents more than a little joy, all the more so because it did not normally last long, but was quickly superseded by a death-like, leaden sleep, from which the child would then certainly not wake again until the next morning.

Summer and autumn had gone by. One fine morning, when the sail-maker came out into the porch of his house after a good night, the region was wrapped in a mantle of snow. White patches lay in the treetops in the pinewoods which formed a wide circle enclosing the lake and the plain in which the village lay.

The sail-maker chuckled to himself. Winter was his favourite season. Snow reminded him of sugar, sugar of grog; grog in turn roused in him the image of warm, festively lit rooms and brought his thoughts to dwell on the fine festivities which are customarily celebrated in winter.

With a secret joy he looked at the unwieldy boats, which could only be propelled with difficulty, because already a thin crust of ice covered the lake. 'Soon,' he told himself, 'they will be stuck fast, and then happy days will be here again.'

It would be mistaken to regard Herr Kielblock as an inveterate idler; on the contrary, no man could work more diligently than he, so long as there was work to do. However, once the movement of boats, and with it his work, was frozen up for months on end, he didn't take it at all to heart, but saw in leisure a welcome opportunity to make merry on what he had earned.

Puffing smoke from his short pipe, he went down the slope to the edge of the lake and tapped the ice with his foot. It broke unexpectedly with the slightest pressure and the sail-maker, although he had conducted the experiment with every care, almost lost his balance.

He drew back with a coarse oath, after picking up his pipe which he had dropped.

A fisherman who had been watching him called over: 'Tha's thinking o' going skating, sail-maker?'*

* In this story Hauptmann writes the dialogue fairly consistently in the dialect of the region to the south-east of Berlin.

'In a week's time, why not?'

'Then I'll be buying me a new net.'

'What for?'

'So as to fish 'ee out again, for tha'll surely fall in.'

Kielblock laughed good-naturedly. He was about to reply when his wife's voice called him in to breakfast. As he went he told himself that first he had better breakfast over the matter, since cold baths were not exactly one of his passions.

The Kielblock family breakfasted.

The old grandmother drank her coffee by the window. As a footrest she used a green square box which she looked at from time to time anxiously with her half-blind eyes. With long parched hands she now opened the drawer of a little table that stood near her, trembling as she did so, and felt about uncertainly inside it until she found a pfennig between her fingers, which she took out and carefully inserted into the bronze slot of the box at her feet.

Kielblock and his wife watched the manoeuvre and nodded understandingly to one another. Over the taut, withered face of the old woman there stole an expression of secret satisfaction, as always in the morning when she found the coin in the drawer which the married couple only rarely forgot to place there for her.

Only yesterday the young woman had changed another mark into pfennigs for this purpose, showing them to her husband and laughing.

'Mother is a good money-box,' he said, casting a longing glance at the green box. 'Who can tell just what is in there. It's more than a trifle, and when she comes to her end, which God forbid, then it will give us a nice little packet, you can depend on that.'

This remark seemed to go to the young woman's legs: she stood up, swung her skirts, and hummed a melody: *To Africa, to the Cameroons, to Angra Pequeña.**

A sudden loud howling interrupted her; the little brown dog Lotte had ventured too close to the green box and been rewarded with a kick from the old woman. The married couple laughed whole-heartedly, while Lotte crept behind the stove and whimpered, a true picture of misery, with pinched snout and arched back.

The old woman spluttered unintelligible words about 'that beast of a dog', and Kielblock shouted into her half-deaf ears; 'Quite so, Mother. What's that animal doing snuffling about there, that's *your* box; you shall keep it, no-one shall touch it, not even a cat or dog, isn't that right?'

'She's got her wits about her all right,' he said with satisfaction, when shortly afterwards he went out into the farmyard with his wife to watch her feeding the animals, 'we won't lose a bean there, will we, Marie my dear?'

Marie set to work immediately with sacks of bran and fodder-tubs, her sleeves and skirts tucked up in spite of the cold air, and her buxom limbs shone in the sunshine.

Kielblock watched his wife with silent satisfaction, still savouring inwardly the reassurance which his mother's avariciousness gave him with regard to his future. He could not bring himself to settle down to work, so much did he relish the experience of this moment. His small, pleasure-loving eyes roved blissfully over the rosy-hued fat backs of his pigs, which in his mind's eye he already saw cut up into hams, sausages and boiled pork. They

* Popular song of the day, celebrating Germany's acquisition of African colonies.

then surveyed the whole farmyard, sprinkled with fresh
snow, which presented to him the impression of a clean
laid table bearing roast chicken, ducks and geese
splendidly served up, although still alive.

His wife Marie was completely buried in her animals
and poultry. For some considerable time the plaintive
crying of a child had been issuing from the porch, which
in no way distracted her from her task. In her livestock
she saw a principal requisite for her comfortable
existence, in the child nothing more, at present, than a
hindrance to it.

It was carnival time. The family was sitting over its
afternoon coffee. Little Gustav, now about one year old,
was playing on the floor. Pancakes had been made and
the Kielblocks were in highly congenial mood, partly
because of the pancakes, partly because it was Saturday,
but mostly because today they were going to attend a
masked ball being held in the village.

Marie was going as a gardening-girl, and her costume
was already hanging near the massive grey tiled stove
which was radiating a great heat. The fire was not
allowed to go out all day long, as an unusually severe
frost had set in a month before, and had even covered the
lake with a layer of ice, so that fully-laden vehicles could
pass over it without danger.

Grandmother was crouched as usual over her treasure
by the window, and Lotte lay basking in the light of the
fire, curled up in front of the opening of the stove, the
small door of which made a gentle rattling sound from
time to time.

That day's ball was to be the last great entertainment

of the winter, and was naturally to be savoured to the ultimate degree.

Winter had so far passed by in the most pleasant manner. Festivities, dances, feastings at home and in other people's houses had alternated with a few hours of work. But reserves had been used up in the process, and live-stock had appreciably dwindled, matters which could not fail to affect the mood of the married couple.

They readily consoled themselves, however, with the thought that the summer would also come and go again, and as for the particular matter of their empty cash-box, a glance at Grandmother's helped them over that worry.

The green box beneath the old woman's feet had always manifested a great calming power in all situations of the married couple's life. If a pig caught red murrain, they thought of the box and resigned themselves. If sailcloth soared in price, or business fell off, they did the same. If it seemed to both of them that a slight recession in their economy was becoming noticeable, the accumulating burden of their worries was once more dispelled by the thought of the box.

Indeed, such a quantity of intriguing suppositions had been woven about the box that the couple had become accustomed to thinking of the moment at which they would be able to open it as the high-point of their lives.

They had long since decided on the use to which they would put the money it contained. First of all, a small portion of it was to be spent on a pleasure trip of about a week's duration, perhaps to Berlin. They would naturally travel without young Gustav, who could easily be found a home for the period of their journey with a family of their acquaintance in the village of Steben on the other side of the lake.

Whenever they talked about this trip, a veritable pleasure-fever took hold of the couple. The husband considered that it should be turned into another honeymoon, while his wife, basking in the memories of her girlhood, could only speak of Renz's circus, the Hasenheide and other places of entertainment.

As so often before, the subject of this trip had once again been brought up when young Gustav, by means of an unusually amusing piece of behaviour, drew attention away from it and onto himself. He raised his little wrinkled arms into the air as if to say 'Listen', and produced from his grubby little mouth a noise that resembled the croak of a toad.

The parents watched the child's antics for a while, suppressing their mirth with difficulty. Finally, however, it became too much for them. They burst out laughing, so loudly that little Gustav began to cry with fear and even the grandmother turned her expressionless face in their direction.

'There, don't cry now, silly boy, no-one's going to harm thee,' said his mother soothingly, standing in front of the child, already half a gardening-girl, in a red corset. 'What are tha thinking of,' she went on, 'waving your arms in the air like a tightrope walker and pulling a face like mother's brother when he caught a hare in his trap.'

Kielblock, who was busily brushing a yellow frock-coat for the evening, added a laughing explanation: 'The lake,' he said, 'the lake!'

And indeed, through the windows came long-drawn-out, muffled noises, loud at times, then softer, like blasts on a tuba, caused by the water of the lake that was working under its gigantic ice-crust, and which the child had presumably just heard and tried to imitate.

The nearer the evening approached, the jollier the couple became, helping one another to dress and amusing themselves in advance of the party with all sorts of jokes and mad tricks, of which Kielblock had a plentiful store gathered in the course of his long practice in the art of enjoyment. His young wife just could not stop laughing, but a sudden dread came over her when Kielblock showed her an ash-grey painted paper face, which he was putting on, so he said, to make people's flesh creep.

'Put the mask away, I beg thee,' she cried, trembling all over. 'That looks just exactly like a dead corpse that's been lying in t'ground for three weeks.'

But her husband was amused by her fear. Holding the mask between his hands, he ran round and round her, so that whichever way she turned, she had to look at it. In the end this made her furious.

'For God's sake, take that monstrosity away,' she shrieked, stamping her foot, while Kielblock, almost exploding with laughter, fell onto a wooden chair and almost overturned it.

At last they were dressed. He as a cut-throat moneylender in yellow frock-coat, velvet knee-breeches and buckled shoes, and a gigantic cardboard inkwell on his head, in which an equally huge quill-pen sat. She as a gardening-girl, swathed in ivy, with a paper crown of roses in her sleek hair.

The clock pointed to seven, so they could set off on their way.

This time too young Gustav had unfortunately to be taken along, however disturbing it was for the 'gardening-girl'.

The grandmother had very recently suffered a stroke, and they could not put even the slightest burden of work upon her. She could just manage to dress and undress by herself, but her strength was almost completely used up in the process.

They placed a little food for the old woman on the window-sill near the burning lamp, so she could safely be left to her fate until the following morning.

They took leave of her, shouting into her deaf ears: 'We're off!' And soon afterwards the old woman at the window and Lotte by the stove were the only occupants of the little house, which Kielblock had locked up from outside.

The pendulum of the old Black Forest clock swung regularly to and fro, 'tick, tock'. The old woman sat silent or recited a prayer in her sharp voice. Lotte growled from time to time in her sleep, and from outside, loud and clear, came the booming tuba-sounds of the lake, whose icy covering extended like an enormous diamond pane, sparkling white in the full moon, sharply defined between the rearing ink-black, shapeless slopes of the pine-clad hills.

When the Kielblocks entered the ballroom they were greeted with a fanfare.

The 'moneylender' aroused uproar. Gardening-girls, gipsy- and huckster-women fled shrieking to their cavaliers, farm-lads and railway-workers, who had squeezed their ample limbs into Spanish costume and wore ornamental daggers that looked like toothpicks at their sides.

The sail-maker was extraordinarily pleased with the

effect of his disguise. For three hours he enjoyed himself driving whole herds of masked women and girls before him, like a wolf chasing lambs.

'Hey, moneylender my friend,' someone called out to him, 'tha looks just as though tha's been hanged three times over and cut down again.' Another advised him to have a schnaps to make him feel better, for schnaps was good for cholera.

The advice was superfluous, for the 'hanged man' had already consumed a large amount of schnaps. In his death's-head skull it had sparked off a second masked ball which was even madder and wilder than the real one.

He came to feel so warm and happy in this state that to preserve his incognito he would have drunk eternal brotherhood with Death the Reaper himself.

At twelve o'clock all the merrymakers removed their masks. Now Kielblock's friends rushed up to him from all sides, assuring him that they really hadn't recognised him: 'You really are the craziest fellow.'

'Damn you for a crafty 'n', tha gallows-bird!' came the confused chorus.

'We should have guessed,' cried a drunken boat-boy. 'Who else but the sail-maker has three skins and is always getting up to tricks?'

Everyone laughed.

'It's the sail-maker, of course, the sail-maker,' they repeated to one another and, as so often before, he again felt himself the hero of the evening.

'Nothing finer,' he shouted into the throng, 'than playing dead for a wee while, but now I'm fed up with it. On we go, music, music!' And his cry found an echo in all throats.

'Music, music, music,' came a medley of shouts, louder and louder, until with a sharp jolt and in shrill discord the band set to work.

The shouting ceased, in a trice the room was filled with whirling figures.

Kielblock danced as though possessed. He stamped with his foot, he bellowed louder than the music.

'Got to show people I'm still alive and kicking,' he bawled to the double-bass player as he shot past the man, who had given him a friendly smile.

Marie forced herself not to cry out, so tight did he hold her: she had almost lost control of her senses. It was as though her husband had become disgusted with his 'death-play' and was now plunging back into life with every fibre of his being.

During the intervals in the music he filled himself with schnaps and treated his friends to it also.

'Drink up, brothers,' he finally babbled, 'ye'll not get me bankrupt, that old mother o' mine has pots of money! Heaps and heaps of it,' he repeated in an emphatic tone, meaningfully winking his eyes and lifting a liquor-glass brim-filled with ginger-brandy unsteadily to his mouth.

The entertainment had passed its peak and threatened to come to an end. Little by little the majority of the guests melted away. Kielblock and spouse and a number of others similarly-minded neither wavered nor yielded. Little Gustav had fortunately been accommodated this time in a dark ante-room, so that he was less of a hindrance than usual.

When even the musicians had gone, someone suggested playing cards, 'God's blessing on Cohen',* a

* Card game played for money.

suggestion which was unanimously taken up. During the game a number of players went to sleep, among them Kielblock.

As soon as the first light of morning stole, pale and ghostly, through the curtains, the couple were awakened. Coming to his senses, the sail-maker bellowed to its close the song over which he had fallen asleep.

'Folks,' he shouted, as it became steadily lighter, 'we ain't a-going home – right?! Not now for sure, when it's getting daylight.'

A few protested; that really was enough now, they shouldn't overdo things! The other half agreed with him.

But what to do?

The inn on the heath was mentioned.

'Yes, folks, let's go on an excursion into the country; if there's a bit of snow lying around it won't hurt us, we'll go together to the inn on the heath.'

'Fresh air, fresh air!' shouted many throats in unison, and they all crowded to the door.

The sun ushered in a Sunday. It hung, a giant piece of yellow-glowing metal, behind the coal-black columns of a pine-wood which, a few hundred paces from the guest-house, projected towards the lake. A brownish golden haze poured through the trunks, penetrating all the gaps in the dark, immobile needle-masses of the treetops, diffusing a reddish light over earth and sky. The air was bitingly cold, but no snow was lying.

The company breathed in the sobering air and shook the smell of the ballroom from their clothes. Some who shortly before had been against the continuation of the occasion now felt themselves so fortified that they spoke in favour of the idea. Others thought it all very well, but must at least change their clothes, if they weren't to make a scandal of themselves. Nobody could find any serious objection to this; and for this reason and the further one that some of those present, including the Kielblocks, declared there were a few things they simply had to attend to, it was decided to go home first of all, but to meet again at nine o'clock to proceed on the outing together.

The Kielblocks departed first, and among those who remained there were few who did not envy the young couple. Statements such as 'If only we could be like that' and so on were expressed as everyone watched the ever-merry man, carrying little Gustav on his arm and holding his wife's hand, disappear into the wood with hearty shouts.

At home everything was in excellent order. Lotte greeted the homecomers, while the old woman still lay in bed. They made coffee for her, woke her and informed her that they would be leaving again shortly. She began to complain to herself, without addressing anybody directly. They managed to calm her with two new pfennig-pieces.

Marie, who was busy changing young Gustav, suddenly became moody. 'Oh blow it, I've had enough,' she said, 'let's stay at home.'

Kielblock was furious.

'I've got a headache and twinges in the back.'

A cup of strong black coffee would cure all that, he declared. They would have to go, for it was they who had started the whole thing off.

The coffee did its job. Young Gustav was wrapped up and everything ready for departure when a boatman appeared who wanted a sail mended by Monday morning. It was for the ice-yacht *Mary*, which was to compete in the big regatta at noon on the following day, he added.

Kielblock declined the job. For the sake of the few coppers that this sort of work produced it wasn't worth depriving oneself of one's bit of Sunday pleasure.

The man assured him that it would be well paid, but Kielblock persisted in his refusal. Work-days were work-days, and rest-days were rest-days.

As they talked business they left the room and the house. He would patch up the sail himself, the boatman concluded, if he could only get the necessary canvas. Even this Kielblock refused, because, as he said, he couldn't allow his preserves to be trespassed upon.

The company met in front of the guest-house. The excursion turned out to be an exceptionally enjoyable one, as the sun had diminished the cold. The husbands flirted with one another's wives, sang, made jokes, and jumped about like stags over the hard-frozen, crackling moss on the forest floor. The woodland echoed with the bawling, shrieking and laughing of the party, whose merriment increased from minute to minute, as they had not forgotten to take a few bottles of brandy along with them to ward off the cold.

At the inn another dance was naturally improvised; towards midday, decidedly lower in spirits, they started on their way back.

It was two o'clock when the Kielblocks arrived back at their little house, somewhat tired and jaded, but by no means satiated. The sail-maker, inserting the key into the door-lock, toyed nevertheless with the thought of turning back. Within him there yawned a great emptiness which he dreaded.

Then his gaze fell upon the lake, which sparkled in the sun like an enormous mirror, animated by skaters and hand-sledges, and an idea occurred to him.

'Marie my dear,' he asked, 'how about making another trip? Over to your sister in Steben – what d'you say? To go and have a nap now, in the middle of the day, that'd be sinful.'

The young woman was too tired, she protested that she couldn't go any further.

'Don't tha worry about that,' replied Kielblock, and ran instantly to the shed behind the house, from which he fetched a green-painted wooden hand-sledge.

'This is the way to do it, I reckon,' he continued, already busy fastening onto his feet a pair of skates which had been hanging over the support of the sledge.

Before Marie had time to voice further doubts, she was sitting there in the sledge holding young Gustav in her lap, speeding over the sparkling sheet of ice, propelled by the powerful arms of her husband.

Scarcely forty metres from the shore the young woman turned and caught sight of the boatman knocking at their door. He must have seen them returning home and decided to call on them once more about the sail.

She drew her husband's attention to him.

He stopped, turned round and broke into resounding laughter which his wife could not resist either. It really was too comical, to see the man standing on the doorstep with his sail, so utterly patient and optimistic, while the people whom he thought were in the house were speeding across the lake behind his back.

Kielblock said it was a good job he hadn't met the man again, otherwise the sleigh trip would have been soured.

As they travelled on he kept turning his head back to see if the man was still standing at his post; but it was only as he climbed up the far bank with his wife and child that he saw him, now no more than a black dot, going away slowly in the direction of the village.

The relatives, who owned a guest-house in Steben, were pleased to have a visit from the couple, especially as a number of other good friends were already present. They were well received, given coffee, pancakes, and later spirits as well. Finally the men got up a game of cards, while the women exchanged gossip. Apart from the circle of relatives there were a few townsfolk present in the guest-room. But they broke up in a hurry when it began to grow dark.

'There's a full moon, ladies and gentlemen,' observed the host, as he pocketed the takings from a small skating party, 'and the lake crossing is completely safe. You don't need to hurry.'

They assured him that they weren't in the least worried, without, however, allowing their leave-taking to be hindered.

'Timid townies,' Kielblock whispered to his brother-in-law, who sat down beside him with a sigh to resume the interrupted game. Raising his umpteenth glass of beer, he called on him to drink, and half-drained his own glass.

'It's true, isn't it,' one of the women called over to the men's table, 'the lad's quite well again now?'

'Quite well,' came the reply. 'Two hours after he was lucky enough to be pulled out and lay safely tucked up in his bed, he suddenly shouted: "Help, help, I'm drowning!"'

'Help, help, I'm drowning,' cried Kielblock, on whom

the beer was again starting to have an effect, and slammed a final card down on the table-top. He won, and smirked as he gathered a number of small coins into the hollow of his hand.

In the meantime someone recounted how a boy had got into the open water of the lake in broad daylight, and would certainly have drowned if some workmen had not chanced to come along at the last moment. All those present knew the spot; it was at the southern tip of the lake, where the slightly warmer water of a little brook ran in.

There was all the more surprise over the accident because this spot did not form a deceptive top covering of ice, but always remained open. The boy must really have gone into it with his eyes shut, the company considered.

Kielblock had won so much that, in the best of moods, he voiced the conviction that he had recouped all his losses of the masked ball. And so without further objections he acceded to his wife's requests that they should now finally be on their way.

Leave-taking of their friends took a long time. They had to discuss hurriedly a little dance-gathering for the following Sunday. Kielblock obtained the promise of all those present to join in the occasion. Everyone agreed, and finally dispersed.

The Kielblocks took the road to the bank of the lake.

Vertically above the blue expanse of ice stood the full moon; it seemed fixed in the sky like the silver ball on top of a gigantic, bespangled crystal dome. A veil of light flowed from it, and magically enwrapped all earthly objects. Air and ground seemed frozen into numbness.

Marie, with the child, had already been sitting on the sledge for some time while Kielblock, cursing all the

42

time, fiddled with his skates. His hands were going dead, he couldn't get them fixed. Little Gustav was crying.

Frau Kielblock urged her husband to hurry; the air was pricking her like needles. Kielblock was well aware of this: it seemed as though the skin on his own face and hands was being scoured with glazier's diamonds.

At last he felt the irons firm beneath his soles. But he still could not grip the sledge; he therefore thrust his hands into his pockets in order to thaw them out a little. In the meantime he executed a few movements on the ice. It was hard, dry and transparent as glass.

'We'll be over in ten minutes,' he said reassuringly, setting the sledge in motion with a powerful heave.

The conveyance sped away across the ice, in a direct line with the yellow light that came from a window of the Kielblocks' house on the opposite side of the lake. It was the grandmother's lamp, which had so often, even on moonless nights, provided the sail-maker with a safe guide. Travelling in a straight line towards it from the Steben inn ensured having consistently solid ice beneath one's feet all the way.

'A real treat to end with,' Kielblock shouted in a hoarse voice into the ear of his wife, who couldn't answer for the chattering of her teeth. She held little Gustav, who was starting to whimper, tight to her.

The sail-maker seemed really insatiable; for this moonlight trip, despite all the preceding exertions, was completely to his taste. He cut all kinds of silly capers, let the sledge slip from his hands at top speed and shot after it like a falcon after its prey. He threw it about so much, in his sheer high spirits, that his wife screamed in protest.

Clearer and clearer grew the outline of their house; already they could make out the individual windows, could distinguish Grandmother in the light of her lamp, when suddenly all became dark.

Kielblock turned in fright and saw a huge wall of cloud, spanning the entire horizon, which had come up unnoticed behind him, and had just engulfed the round full moon.

'I must hurry now,' he said and pushed the sledge with redoubled speed before him over the ice.

The house was still lit by the moon; but the giant cloud-shadow crept further and further across the lake, until both lake and house were cloaked in impenetrable darkness.

Kielblock steered unperturbed for the shining light which came from the grandmother's lamp. He told himself that he had nothing to fear, but was impelled to hurry by an invisible power.

He gathered all his strength together: the sweat streamed from every pore; his body burned: he panted for breath . . .

His young wife sat hunched up, holding the child pressed to her convulsively. She spoke no word, she did not move, as though fearful that she might lessen their travelling speed. Her breast was likewise gripped by an inexplicable feeling of anxiety; her only wish was to be at the end of their journey.

Meanwhile it had grown so black that Kielblock could no longer see his wife, nor she her child. At the same time the lake rumbled continuously under its covering of ice. There was a shuffling and grumbling, then a dull, suppressed roar, accompanied by a surging against the ice-sheet, causing it to burst explosively in great fissures.

Custom had dulled Kielblock's sensitivity towards the uncanny quality of the phenomenon; now it suddenly seemed to him as though he were standing on top of an enormous cage, in which were incarcerated hordes of bloodthirsty beasts of prey, roaring with hunger and rage, sinking their claws and teeth into the walls of their prison.

On all sides came the sound of fissures cracking through the ice.

Kielblock had grown up by the lake, he knew that with an ice-sheet twelve inches thick, falling through was an impossibility. But his imagination began to roam and no longer entirely obeyed his sober judgement. At times it seemed as though black abysses were opening under him, to engulf him with wife and child.

A rumbling like thunder rolled towards him from the distance and finished in a muffled clap directly below his feet.

His wife screamed.

He was about to ask her if she had gone mad when he noticed something that drove the words back into his throat. The only point of light that had guided him so far was moving – becoming dimmer and dimmer – flared up – flickered – and completely disappeared.

'For God's sake, what's mother thinking of!' he exclaimed involuntarily, and like a flash of lightning the consciousness of real danger passed through his brain.

He had stopped and rubbed his eyes; was it reality or only deception? He almost believed it was the latter; the image on his retina was deceiving him. Finally this too dispersed, and now he felt as if he were drowned in darkness. Still he believed that he knew the exact direction in which the extinguished light lay, and travelled towards it swift as an arrow.

Amid the turbulence of the lake he heard his wife's

voice penetrating to him through the darkness, throwing all sorts of reproaches at him; why hadn't they stayed at home, and so forth.

Several minutes went by. At last they thought they heard dogs barking. Kielblock heaved a sigh of relief. Then a desperate cry – a jolt – the sparks flew from under his skates; with almost superhuman strength he heaved the sledge about and stopped.

His wife's right arm clasped his own, trembling and convulsive. He knew that she had seen death.

'Keep calm, Marie dearest, it's nothing,' he said comfortingly in a quivering voice, and yet it seemed to him also as though a snow-cold, dead hand had plucked at his hot heart.

His young wife was trembling like an aspen: her tongue seemed lamed. 'Oh! Oh! . . . my God! . . . my God!' was all that she could bring forth.

'What in heaven's name is the matter, girl, tell me, for God's sake, tell me!'

'There . . . there . . . ,' she exclaimed, 'I heard it . . . quite clearly . . . water . . . water . . . open water!'

He listened intently. 'I can't hear anything!'

'I saw it, truly, I saw it, clearly I did . . . right in front of me . . . truly.'

Kielblock tried to pierce the dense air with his gaze – in vain. He felt as though his eyes had been removed from his head and he was endeavouring to see with the sockets. 'I can't see anything.'

His wife calmed herself a little. 'But there's the smell of water.'

He told her she had been dreaming, and yet felt his own anxiety growing.

Little Gustav was sleeping.

He started to go ahead slowly; but his wife countered with all the strength of deadly fear. In weeping tones she implored him to turn round; when he did not halt, she behaved like a lunatic: 'It's cracking, it's cracking!'

Now his patience snapped. He shouted at his wife that she would be responsible, with her accursed lamentations, if he were to be drowned together with her and the child. She should keep her mouth shut, or, as sure as his name was Kielblock, he would leave her to herself in the middle of the lake. When all this did no good, he lost his sense of reason and babbled all kinds of stupid things. In addition to this he now really did not know which was his right direction. But the spot on which he was standing seemed to him brittle and unsafe. Vainly he tried to master the dreadful anguish which was beginning to take control of him too. Fantasies filled his brain, he trembled, he gasped out fervent prayers: was this really and truly to be the end of everything? Here today, gone tomorrow – he had never understood it. Here today, gone tomorrow – tomorrow – gone – what did it mean, 'gone'? Up to now he had not known, but now – no, no!

A cold terror seized him, he turned the sledge, he took a run-up with one last, almighty exertion of his strength – rescue at all price, and now – a splashing sound, a gushing, foaming and frothing of displaced masses of water – he lost consciousness.

A moment, and he knew that he had gone straight into the open stretch of the lake. His powerful limbs threshed in the black water: he trod the ice-cold wetness with superhuman strength, until he felt that he could breathe again.

A cry escaped from his breast, echoing afar – a second

one – a third, almost bursting his lungs, shattering his larynx; he shuddered at the sound from his own throat, but he shouted – he bellowed like an animal: 'Help, help us – we're drowning – Help!'

Then with a gurgling sound he went under and the cry with him, until he came up again and yelled once more.

He raised his right hand out of the water; still shouting, he looked for a handhold – in vain; once more he went down. When he came up it was light around him. About three arm-lengths to his left the ice-cap began, extending in a great arc around an area of open water. He struggled to reach it. Once more he sank, but at last he gripped it, his fingers slipped off, he tried again and dug them in as if they were claws – he pulled himself up. As far as his shoulders he was above water, his eyes staring in fear close to the ice-sheet that now burned white again in the moonshine. There – there was his house – further off the village, and there, sure enough, lanterns – lights – rescue! Again his shout quavered through the night.

He listened intently.

From high in the air came a sound. Wild geese swept across the vault of the stars and then as single dark points across the full moon. Behind him he heard a gurgling and seething of the waters. Bubbles rose, he felt his blood run chill; he shuddered to turn round, yet he turned. A dark mass surged to the surface and sank again at intervals. A shoe, a hand, a fur cap became visible; it all swirled closer and closer, he tried to seize hold of it, but it sank again.

A moment of mortal fear – then mad laughter. He felt something fastening about him from below; first it seized his foot – then it entwined his legs – it rose as far as his heart – his eyes became glazed – his hands slipped away – he sank – muffled distant humming – a blurr of images and thoughts – then – death.

The cry for help had been heard in the village.

Labourers and fishermen gathered at the scene of the mishap. After the passage of an hour they hauled the corpse of a child onto the ice. They concluded from his age that an adult must also have been drowned.

When further searching produced no result, a fisherman suggested that they should put nets down. And so, at about three o'clock in the morning, the nets also brought up the bodies of the young couple.

There lay the merry sail-maker with distorted, bloated features, arraigning the malice of heaven with his sightless eyes. His clothes dripped, from his pockets flowed black pools of water. As they lifted him onto the stretcher, a number of small coins fell jingling on the ice.

The three corpses were recognised and conveyed to the Kielblocks' house.

The door was found locked; no light shone from the windows. A dog was barking inside, but even after repeated knocking, no-one opened the door. A fisherman climbed through the window into the dark living-room; his lantern only half-illuminated it, it was empty. Making a loud noise in his wading-boots, barked at by a small brown dog, he strode straight across the room and came to a small door which he immediately pushed open. He uttered a cry of astonishment.

In the centre of a windowless alcove sat a very old woman; she had dozed off over a green box which stood open on the floor, and was filled with gold, silver and copper coins. Her right hand was buried above the knuckles in the metal, her face rested on her left hand. Over her almost bald head the meagre flame of the burned-down lamp cast a hazy, wan light.

Lineman Thiel

I

Every Sunday the railwayman Thiel took his seat in the church at Neu-Zittau, except for those days when he was on duty or was ill in bed. In the course of ten years he had been ill twice; once as the result of being struck by a piece of coal that fell from the tender of a passing engine, throwing him into the ditch beside the track with a smashed leg; the other time it was a wine-bottle, which had hit him plumb in the chest as it flew from an express train roaring by. Apart from these two accidents, nothing had been able to keep him away from church as soon as he was off-duty.

For the first five years he had walked alone from Schön-Schornstein, a settlement on the Spree, over to Neu-Zittau. Then one fine day he made his appearance in the company of a lean and somewhat sickly-looking young woman, who, it was generally considered, was a poor match for his herculean figure. And on a further fine Sunday afternoon at the altar of the church, he solemnly bound himself for life to this same person. Then for two years the delicate young woman sat at his side in the pew; for two years her thin, hollow-cheeked face peered beside his own weather-beaten features into the ancient hymn-book; and suddenly the lineman sat there alone again, as before.

One day in the previous week the bell had tolled for a death: that was all.

Hardly any change had been noticed in the rail-wayman, people asserted. The buttons on his clean Sunday uniform were polished as brightly as ever before, his red hair as well oiled and given its military parting as usual; it was just possible to detect that he hung his broad, hairy neck a little and that he listened to the sermon or sang more assiduously than he had done before. The general opinion was that the death of his wife had not affected him closely; and this view was strengthened when, after an interval of a year, Thiel married once more, this time a fat, sturdy creature who was a milk-maid from Alte-Grund.

Even the parson allowed himself to express some misgivings when Thiel came to announce the engagement.

'So you're thinking of marrying again already?'

'I can't keep house with the one that's dead, parson!'

'Well, yes, that's true – but I mean – aren't you rather hurrying things?'

'It's the boy I'm concerned about, parson.'

Thiel's wife had died in childbed, and the boy whom she had brought into the world lived and was given the name Tobias.

'Ah, yes, the boy,' said the minister and made a gesture which showed clearly that he had only just remembered the little one. 'That's a different matter – who looks after him now while you're on duty?'

Thiel recounted how he had entrusted Tobias to an old woman who had once almost allowed him to burn himself, while on another occasion he had tumbled off her lap onto the ground, fortunately with no more than a large bruise to show for it. Things couldn't go on like that any longer, he said, especially since the boy, not being very strong, needed very special care and attention. For this reason, and for the additional one that he had faithfully promised his dead wife that he would at all times attend with particular care to the well-being of the boy, he had decided to take this step.

Towards the new couple, who now attended church every Sunday, people had no outward objection at all. The former milk-maid seemed to have been made for the railwayman. She was scarcely half a head shorter in height and surpassed him in physique. Her face, too, was every bit as coarse in its features as was his, except that, in contrast to Thiel's, hers lacked all soul.

If Thiel had cherished the hope of possessing in his second wife an indefatigable worker and an exemplary housekeeper, then his hope had been fulfilled to an astonishing degree. But he had also, without knowing it, taken on three things into the bargain: a hard, domineering temperament, a quarrelsome nature, and a brutish violence of temper. After the passage of half a year it was known all over the neighbourhood who called the tune in the railwayman's house. People felt sorry for him.

It had been lucky for the 'creature' that she had found such a good sheep as Thiel for her husband, said the married men indignantly: there were some with whom she would have come into headlong conflict. It must be possible to tame such an 'animal', though, they reckoned – with blows, if all else failed. She needed a good thrashing, one that would really leave its mark.

But in spite of his sinewy arms Thiel was not the man to give her a thrashing. What agitated these people seemed to cause him very little worry. He usually allowed his wife's endless sermons to pass over him without a word, and when he did occasionally answer, the laboured pace and cool, gentle tone of his speech stood in strange contrast to the screeching invective of his wife. The external world seemed to have little impact on him; it was as though he had a store of goodness within him with which he cancelled out all wrongs that it did him.

Despite his indestructible phlegm, however, he had moments when he would not be trifled with. This was always so in matters that concerned young Tobias. His childishly naive, easy-going nature then acquired a degree of tenacity which even such an untamed spirit as Lena's did not dare to oppose.

However, the moments in which he revealed this side of his nature became more and more infrequent and eventually disappeared altogether. A certain passive resistance with which he had countered the domineering spirit of Lena during the first year likewise vanished in the course of the second. No longer did he go on duty with his erstwhile imperturbability after a scene with her, if he had not first pacified her. And finally he not infrequently lowered himself to begging her to be nice again. No longer now was his lonely post in the midst of the Brandenburg pine-forest his favourite resort. His silent, devout reflection on his dead wife was crossed with thoughts of his living one. It was not with reluctance, as in the early days, that he set off on his way home, but with a passionate haste, often following hours and minutes of counting off the time for the arrival of his relief.

This man who had been bound to his first wife

primarily by a spiritual love now placed himself, through the force of base instincts, in the power of his second wife, and in the end became almost totally dependent on her in every respect. There were times when he experienced pangs of conscience at this volte-face, and he resorted to a number of extraordinary measures to get over them. Thus he secretly declared his lineman's hut and the section of permanent way that he had to attend to to be a kind of sacred realm, dedicated solely and exclusively to the shades of the dead. Using all sorts of pretexts, he had actually succeeded so far in keeping his wife from accompanying him there.

It was his hope to be able to continue to do so. She would not have known which direction to take to find his hut, whose number she did not even know.

By thus conscientiously dividing up the time at his disposal between the living and the dead Thiel was actually able to still his conscience.

Often, to be sure, and especially in moments of lonely devotions, when he had entered into profoundest communion with the dead, he saw his present condition in the light of truth and was nauseated by it.

If he was on duty during the day, then he restricted his spiritual contact with the dead to a number of sweet memories from the time when they had lived together. But in darkness, when a snow-storm raged through the pines and across the track, in the depths of midnight by the light of his lantern, his hut became a chapel.

A faded photograph of the dead woman in front of him on the table, hymn-book and bible opened wide, he read and sang in turn throughout the long night, interrupted only by the railway trains that roared past at intervals, and so arrived at a state of ecstasy, rising to visionary heights in which he saw his dead wife physically before him.

The post that the lineman had now occupied without a break for a good ten years had through its remoteness the effect of feeding his mystical inclinations.

Lying at least three-quarters of an hour distant from human habitation in any direction, his hut stood in the midst of the forest, close to a crossing whose barriers the lineman had to operate.

In summer whole days went past, and in winter entire weeks, without a single human foot passing by this section of the track apart from the lineman and his colleague. The weather and the changes of the seasons, in their periodic return, produced almost the only variation in this wilderness. The events which had otherwise punctuated the regular passing of Thiel's hours of duty, apart from his two accidents, were not difficult to review. Four years previously the special imperial train, which was carrying the Emperor to Breslau, had swept by. One winter's night the express had run over a stag. One hot summer's day Thiel had found a bottle of wine with its cork still intact during his inspection of the track; it was burning hot to the touch and he regarded its contents as very good, since they spurted forth like a fountain when the cork was removed, showing that they had obviously fermented. This bottle, which he had placed for cooling in the shallows of a woodland pool, had somehow gone astray, leaving Thiel to lament its loss for some years afterwards.

A well just behind his house provided some interest in the lineman's life. From time to time rail or telegraph workers who were operating in the neighbourhood took a drink from it, which of course became the occasion for a short conversation. The forester was another person who sometimes came to quench his thirst.

Tobias made slow progress in his development: it was only towards the end of his second year that he acquired any sort of ability to walk and speak. He was especially attached to his father. As his understanding grew, his father's earlier affection for him reawakened. In proportion to the increase of Thiel's affection, that of his stepmother diminished progressively and even turned to undisguised aversion when at the end of a further year Lena gave birth to a boy.

From then on a bad time started for Tobias. He was incessantly put upon, especially in his father's absence, and was made to apply his feeble powers in the service of the bawling infant, without the slightest reward, so that he increasingly wore himself out. His head acquired unconventional proportions: his flaming red hair and the chalk-coloured face beneath it made an unappealing, pitiful impression in conjunction with the rest of his sorry shape. When the retarded Tobias struggled down to the Spree with his little brother in his arms, radiating health and vigour, imprecations were loud behind the windows of the village houses, never, however, to be repeated outside the walls. But Thiel, who after all was the one most concerned, seemed not to notice, and ignored the hints given him by well-intending neighbours.

II

One June morning at about seven o'clock Thiel came off duty. His wife had scarcely finished greeting him before she began, in customary fashion, to complain. The lease of the piece of land that the family rented to meet its needs in potatoes had been terminated some weeks ago, and Lena had been unable to find a substitute for it. Although looking after this piece of land was one of Lena's responsibilities, Thiel was nevertheless informed time and time again that he and he alone was to blame if they had to buy ten sacks of potatoes for hard cash this year. Thiel merely growled and, paying little attention to Lena's words, went over to the older boy's bed, which he shared with him on the nights when he was not on duty. Here he lay down, studied the sleeping child with an anxious expression on his good face, and after chasing away the persistent flies from him for a time, finally roused him. An expression of pathetic joy filled the blue, deep-set eyes of the waking boy. He hurriedly seized hold of his father's hand, while the corners of his mouth puckered into a pitiful smile. The lineman immediately helped him to put on his few items of clothing, and something like a shadow suddenly flashed across his features as he noticed on the slightly swollen right cheek the white-in-red imprint of finger-marks.

When, at breakfast, Lena came back with greater energy than ever to the domestic matter that she had raised before, he cut her short with the news that the permanent way inspector had assigned to him, free of charge, a piece of land alongside the track and quite near his hut, on the grounds that it was too remote for the inspector himself.

At first Lena wouldn't believe it. Gradually, however, her doubts disappeared, and then she became markedly good-tempered. Her questions about the size and quality of the plot of land and so on poured out precipitately, and when she discovered that there were two dwarf fruit trees on it into the bargain, she became quite crazed. When there was nothing more to ask about, and as the doorbell of the local store, which incidentally could be heard in every single house of the vicinity, was ringing incessantly, she darted away to scatter her news among the neighbours.

While Lena was away in the dark depths of the general store, crammed with its wares, the lineman stayed at home, devoting his attention entirely to Tobias. The boy sat on his knees and played with some pinecones that Thiel had brought with him from the woods.

'What are you going to be?' his father asked him, and this question was as stereotyped as the boy's reply: 'A Permanent Way Inspector'.* It was not just a game, for the lineman's dreams aspired indeed to such heights, and he cherished in all seriousness the desire and the hope that with God's help Tobias would achieve something extraordinary. As soon as the response 'A Permanent Way Inspector' came from the bloodless lips of the boy, who naturally had no idea what the words meant, Thiel's face began to brighten, until it quite shone with an inner rapture.

'Off you go, Tobias, go and play!' he then said briefly, lighting his pipe with a splint of wood which he kindled in the stove, and the boy slipped immediately out of doors filled with a shy sense of joy. Thiel undressed, went to bed and fell asleep, after gazing reflectively for some

---

* The German railways divided their employees at this time into seventeen different salary and wage groups. A *Bahnwärter* – lineman, like Thiel, was in the lowest, group 17; a *Bahnmeister* – permanent way inspector, was in the comparatively high group 7.

time at the low, cracked ceiling of the room. At about noon he woke up, dressed and, while his wife prepared the mid-day meal in her usual clattering way, went out into the street where he immediately took charge of young Tobias, who was digging lime out of a hole in the wall with his fingers and putting it into his mouth. The lineman took his hand and walked with him past the eight or so little houses of the settlement down to the Spree, whose waters lay dark and glassy between lines of sparse poplars. At the very edge of the river stood a block of granite, on which Thiel seated himself.

The whole neighbourhood had grown used to seeing him at this point whenever the weather made it at all possible. The children above all were very attached to him, calling him 'Father Thiel', and in particular learned quite a number of games from him, which he remembered from his own youth. But he reserved the best of his recollections for Tobias. He cut tapering arrows for him which flew higher than those of all the other boys. He made little willow pipes for him and even went to the length of singing the incantation appropriate to this task, in his rusty bass voice, while he carefully tapped the bark with the horn handle of his pocket-knife.

The local people held these inconsequentialities against him; they just did not understand how he could give so much time to the snotty-nosed creatures. Actually, however, they had cause to be satisfied with this state of affairs, for under his supervision the children were in safe hands. Besides, Thiel did serious things with them, too, heard the bigger ones recite their school homework, helped them learn their pieces from the bible or hymn-books, and with the little ones practised their spelling; t–o, to; o–n, on, and so forth.

After the meal the lineman lay down again for a short rest. At the end of it he drank his mid-afternoon coffee and immediately set about preparing himself for going on duty. For this, as for all his undertakings, he required plenty of time; every gesture was executed in accordance with a years-old ritual; in the same unvarying sequence the objects that he had laid out carefully on the walnut chest of drawers – knife, note-book, comb, a horse's tooth, his old encased pocket-watch – found their way into the pockets of his clothes. A little book in a red paper wrapper was handled with particular care. During the night it lay beneath the lineman's pillow, and in the daytime was always carried about in the breast-pocket of his uniform. On a label underneath the wrapper there stood in clumsy but ornamental lettering an inscription in Thiel's own hand: Savings Book of Tobias Thiel.

The wall-clock with the long pendulum and jaundiced face was pointing to a quarter to five as Thiel set off. A small boat which he owned carried him across the river. On the far bank of the Spree he stood still a few times, listening for sounds from the village. At length he turned into a broad woodland track and after a few minutes was surrounded by the deep surging of the pine forest, whose massed branches were like a dark green, undulating sea. Noiselessly, as if on felt, he walked over the damp woodland carpet of moss and pine-needles. He found his way without looking up, here between the rust-brown columns of the older trees, there through young growth densely intertwined, then again through extensive stretches of new planting lying in the shade of a few tall, slender pines that had been left as a protection for the new trees. A bluish, transparent haze, impregnated with all manner of scents, rose from the ground, blurring the shapes of the trees. A heavy, milky sky hung low over the tree-tops. Flocks of crows bathed, as it were, in the greyness of the air, ceaselessly emitting their jarring calls. Black patches of water filled the hollows in the track and reflected an even gloomier image of a gloomy natural scene.

Dreadful weather, thought Thiel, waking from his deep reflection and looking about him.

Suddenly his thoughts turned in another direction. He had a vague feeling that he must have left something behind him at home, and on going through his pockets he did in fact discover the absence of the sandwiches which he always had to take with him because of his long hours of duty. For a short time he stood irresolute, but then suddenly turned and hurried back towards the village.

He had soon reached the Spree, crossed it with a few powerful strokes of the oars, and at once set off up the gently sloping village street, his body bathed in sweat. The storekeeper's bedraggled old poodle lay in the middle of the street. On the tarred board fence of a small-holding sat a hooded crow. It spread its feathers, shook itself, nodded, uttered an ear-splitting 'kra-kra' and rose with a sharp whistle of its wings, to be borne away by the wind in the direction of the forest.

Of the inhabitants of this little colony, about twenty fishermen and forestry workers with their families, nothing was to be seen.

The sound of a shrieking voice broke the silence so loudly and shrilly that the lineman involuntarily stopped in his tracks. A flood of violently ejaculated, discordant notes struck his ear, coming, it appeared, from the open gable window of a low-built house which he knew only too well.

Muffling the sound of his footsteps as far as possible, he crept closer and could now make out quite distinctly the voice of his wife. A few more paces, and the majority of her words became intelligible.

'What, you unfeeling, heartless wretch! Is the poor little thing to cry his heart out with hunger? – what? Just you wait, now, just you wait, I'll teach you to pay attention! You'll get something to remember.' For a few moments there was silence; then a sound was heard like that of clothes being beaten; it was followed immediately by a new storm of abuse.

'You miserable little runt,' the words rang out in a breathless tempo, 'Do you suppose I'm going to let my own child go hungry for the sake of a wretched creature like you? Shut your mouth!' the voice cried, as a subdued whimpering became audible, 'or you'll get enough to last you a whole week.'

The whimpering did not stop.

The lineman felt his heart beat with a heavy, irregular throb. He began to tremble slightly. He gazed fixedly at the ground, as though elsewhere in his thoughts, and his hard, clumsy hand several times brushed aside a lock of damp hair that kept falling over his freckled brow.

For a moment it almost got the better of him. There was a spasm, which caused his muscles to swell and the fingers of his hand to clench into a fist. It passed, leaving in its wake a dull weariness.

With uncertain tread the lineman entered the narrow, stone-tiled hall of the house. His tired feet slowly mounted the creaking wooden stairs.

'Shame on you! For shame! For shame!' the voice started up again; at the same time came the sound of someone spitting three times in succession in a total manifestation of rage and contempt. 'You pitiful, vile, deceitful, malicious, cowardly, vulgar lout!' The words followed one another with a rising intonation, and the voice that emitted them broke under the strain at times. 'Strike my boy, would you, eh? You miserable brat, you'd dare to hit the poor, defenceless child in the mouth? – What? – Heh? If it wasn't that I didn't want to dirty myself on you, I'd . . .'

At this moment Thiel opened the door of the living-room, causing the rest of the sentence to stick unfinished in the throat of his startled wife. She was white as a sheet with anger; her lips quivered viciously: she had raised her right hand, but let it fall and took hold of the milk jug, from which she attempted to fill a child's feeding-bottle. She left this job half-done, however, as the greater part of the milk ran over the neck of the bottle onto the table, and, quite unable to control herself in her agitation, picked up first one object, then another without being able to hold it for more than a few moments, and finally managed to control herself sufficiently to let fly at her husband: what was the meaning of his coming home at this unaccustomed time, surely he wasn't trying to spy on her? 'That would really be the last straw,' she said, and followed up with the declaration that her conscience was clear and she had no need to avoid anyone's gaze.

Thiel scarcely heard what she was saying. He directed a fleeting look at the howling figure of little Tobias. For a moment it seemed as though he had forcibly to hold back something terrible that rose up in him; then suddenly the old phlegm settled upon his tensed features, strangely animated by a furtive flash of desire in his gaze. For a split second his eyes dwelt on the powerful limbs of his wife, who, bustling about with averted face, was still attempting to control herself. Her ample, half-bared breasts were swollen with agitation and threatened to burst their bodice, and her tucked-up skirts made her broad hips appear even broader. A power seemed to emanate from the woman, invincible, unescapable, to which Thiel felt himself quite unequal.

Gently, like a fine spider's web, and yet tight as a mesh of iron, it settled about him, shackling, subduing, enervating. He would not have been capable of directing one word at her in this state, least of all a harsh one, and so Tobias, who was crouching fearfully in a corner, bathed in tears, was forced to witness how his father, without paying further attention to him, took the sandwiches that he had forgotten from the seat by the stove, held them out to his mother in sole explanation, and with a short, absent-minded nod of the head was gone again.

III

Although Thiel covered the distance back to the solitude of his woods as quickly as he could, it was fifteen minutes past the regulation time when he arrived at his place of duty.

The assistant lineman, a man who had become consumptive in consequence of the unavoidably rapid changes of temperature associated with his work, and who took turns with him in duties, was already standing ready to leave on the small sandy platform of the hut, whose large number, black on white, stood out for quite a

65

distance through the tree-trunks.

The two men shook hands, exchanged a few brief pieces of information and parted. The one disappeared inside the hut, the other crossed straight over the track to use the continuation of the road by which Thiel had come. His convulsive coughing could be heard, at first close at hand, then further off through the trees, and with its cessation the only human sound disappeared from this wilderness. Thiel began, today as always, by arranging the small, square, stone-built lineman's hut in his own way for the night. He did it mechanically, while his mind was occupied with the impact of the last few hours. He put his sandwiches down on the narrow, brown-painted table by one of the two slit-shaped side windows, through which an eye could be comfortably kept on the track. He next lit a fire in the small, rusty stove and placed a pan of cold water on it. Finally, after doing some tidying of the implements, shovels, spades, vice and so on, he set about cleaning his lamp, which he immediately filled with fresh paraffin.

When this had been done, three shrill bursts on the bell, which were repeated, announced that a train travelling from Breslau had been cleared by the next station down the line. Showing not the slightest sign of haste, Thiel remained a good while yet inside the cabin, finally emerging into the open, flag and detonator-bag in hand, to walk with a lazy, shambling gait along the narrow sandy path to the level-crossing that was about twenty paces distant. Thiel was conscientious in the closing and opening of his barriers before and after each train, although the road was scarcely ever used.

His job finished, he leaned waiting against the black and white barrier.

The track cut a straight line to right and left through the never-ending green of the forest; at either side of it the masses of green foliage seemed to check themselves, leaving a lane free between them, which was taken up by the reddish-brown, gravel-covered permanent way. The black, parallel-lying rails upon it resembled overall a gigantic iron mesh, whose narrow strands coverged at points on the horizon to the extreme south and north.

The wind had risen and stirred the fringe of the wood into gentle waves, passing on into the distance. From the telegraph posts which ran alongside the track came a harmonious humming. To the wires which spun themselves from post to post like the web of some giant spider, flocks of twittering birds clung in serried rows. A woodpecker flew over Thiel's head with its laughing call, unacknowledged by so much as a glance.

The sun, which emerged at that moment beneath a bank of massive clouds to sink into the dark-green sea of crests, poured streams of purple over the forest. The colonnades of pine-trunks on the other side of the track seemed to flame incandescently and glow like iron.

The rails too began to glow, like fiery snakes; but they were the first to die out. And now the glow slowly rose from the ground into the air, leaving first the shafts of the pines and then the greater part of their crowns in the cold stagnant light, until finally only the topmost points of the crests were touched by a reddish shimmer. Silently and solemnly the sublime spectacle was enacted. The lineman was still standing motionless at the barrier. At last he took a step forward. A dark point on the horizon where the lines met was increasing in size. Growing from second to second, it yet seemed to remain in one place. Suddenly it acquired motion and approached. Through the lines there went a vibration and a humming, a rhythmical clatter, a muffled commotion, becoming louder and louder until it was not unlike the pounding of an approaching cavalry squadron.

From the distance a snorting and thundering came in waves through the air. Then suddenly the stillness was rent. A furious raging and roaring filled the whole place, the lines bent, the ground trembled – a mighty pressure of air – a cloud of dust, steam and smoke, and the black, snorting monster was past. Just as they had grown, the sounds gradually died away. The vapour dispersed. Shrunk to a point, the train disappeared into the distance, and the old sacred silence closed in again over the woods.

'Minna,' whispered the lineman as though waking from a dream, and went back to his hut. After he had brewed himself some weak coffee he sat down and, taking a mouthful from time to time, gazed at a dirty piece of newspaper that he had picked up somewhere along the track.

Gradually a strange restlessness came over him. He put it down to the heat of the stove which filled the small room, and opened up his jacket and waistcoat to make himself easier. When that didn't help, he rose, took a spade from the corner, and made his way to the plot that he had been given.

It was a narrow strip of sand, thickly overgrown with weeds. Like snow-white foam the splendour of the spring blossom lay on the branches of the two dwarf fruit-trees that stood on it.

Thiel grew calm, and a feeling of quiet contentment

came over him.

Now then, to work!

The spade cut into the ground with a grating sound, the damp clods fell back again with a dull thud and broke apart.

For a time he dug without interruption. Then he suddenly stopped and said to himself, loud and clear, as he moved his head dubiously from side to side: 'No, no, that won't do,' and again, 'No, no, that won't do at all.'

It had suddenly occurred to him that Lena would now come out frequently to tend the plot, which meant that his customary mode of life was bound to experience serious disturbances. And his joy over the possession of the land turned abruptly to repugnance. Hurriedly, as though he had been on the point of doing something wrong, he pulled his spade out of the earth and carried it back to the hut. Here he sank again into dark brooding. He scarcely knew why, but the prospect of having Lena with him on duty for entire days on end grew more and more unbearable, however much he tried to reconcile himself to the idea. He had the feeling that there was something precious to him that he must defend, as though someone were trying to get at his most sacred possession, and his muscles tautened involuntarily in a mild spasm, while a short, defiant laugh issued from his lips. Frightened by the echo of this laugh, he looked up and lost the thread of his reflections. When he found it again, he burrowed back deep into the old theme.

And suddenly something like a dense black curtain was torn asunder, and his bemused eyes saw clearly. He felt all at once as though he were waking up from two years of death-like sleep, and surveyed with an incredulous shaking of the head all the dire things that he had committed in this condition. The tribulations of his elder boy, on which the impressions of the last few hours had merely set the seal, presented themselves clearly to his soul. Pity and remorse seized him, and a deep sense of shame that he had lived all this time in abject tolerance, without any concern for the dear, helpless creature, indeed without even finding the strength to admit to himself how much the child was suffering.

Under the self-tormenting consciousness of all his sins of omission he was overcome by a deep weariness, and he fell asleep with hunched back, his forehead resting on his hand and his hand on the table.

He had been lying there for some time when he called out the name 'Minna' several times in a choking voice.

A rushing and roaring filled his ears, as if from immeasurable masses of water; it became dark around him, he opened his eyes and woke up. His limbs were trembling, a sweat of anxiety broke from every pore, his pulse beat unevenly, his face was wet with tears.

It was pitch-dark. He tried to look in the direction of the door, but did not know where to turn. He staggered to his feet, the anguish in his heart continuing to rage. The forest outside roared like surf on the sea, the wind threw hail and rain against the windows of the hut. In despair Thiel fumbled about him. For a moment he felt like a drowning man – then suddenly there was a blinding flash of blue light, as though drops of celestial radiance were falling into the dark atmosphere of the earth, to be immediately stifled by it.

This moment sufficed to bring the lineman to his senses. He reached for his lamp, which he was fortunate enough to lay hands on, and at this moment the thunder broke loose at the furthest edge of the Brandenburg night sky. At first muffled and subdued in its rumblings, it rolled nearer in short, surging breakers until, rising to giant proportions, it finally loosed itself, flooding the whole atmosphere with its booming, shattering, raging fury.

The window-panes rattled, the earth trembled.

Thiel had lit a light. His first glance, after he had regained his self-control, was at the clock. Scarcely five minutes separated the present moment from the arrival of the express. Thinking that he had failed to hear the signal, he made his way, as quickly as storm and darkness permitted, to the barrier. While he was still busy closing it, the alarm signal rang. The wind rent its sounds to shreds and scattered them in all directions. The pines bent and rubbed their branches against each other, grating and creaking weirdly. For a moment the moon came into view, looking like a pale golden bowl among the clouds. By its light the wind could be seen burrowing among the dark crowns of the pines. The trailing foliage of the birches by the permanent way waved and flapped like ghostly horses' tails. Below, the lines of the rails, glistening with wet, concentrated the moon's pale light at scattered points.

Thiel tore his cap from his head. The rain did him good and ran, mingled with tears, down his face. There was a ferment in his brain; vague recollections of what he had seen in his dream pursued one another. It had been as though someone were ill-treating Tobias, and in so frightful a way that his heart stood still even now at the very thought of it. Another impression remained more clearly in his memory. He had seen his dead wife. She had come from somewhere far away, on one of the railway tracks. She had looked really ill, and instead of clothes she had worn rags. She had gone past Thiel's hut without glancing at it, and in the end – here his memory became confused – she had for some reason found the greatest difficulty in continuing on her way and had even collapsed completely several times.

Thiel thought about it further, and now he knew that she had been fleeing. There could be no doubt about it, for why else should she have looked behind her with such expressions of dreadful anxiety, and struggled on although her feet were failing her. Oh, those frightful eyes!

But there was something that she was carrying, wrapped in cloths, something flabby, bloody, pale, and the way in which she looked down at it reminded him of scenes from the past.

He thought of a dying woman, looking steadfastly at her scarce-born child, which she now had to leave behind her, with an expression of deepest grief, of inconceivable agony, that expression which Thiel could no more forget than the fact that he had a mother and father.

Where had she gone? He did not know. But one thing was clear in his mind: she had renounced him, ignored him; she had struggled on further and further through the dark, stormy night. He had called to her: 'Minna, Minna', and that had woken him up.

Two round red lights pierced the darkness like the staring eyes of some enormous monster. A blood-red glow preceded them, transforming the raindrops in its proximity into drops of blood. It was as though the heavens were raining blood.

Thiel experienced a shudder of horror and, as the train came nearer, an ever-growing anxiety; dream and reality fused into one for him. He still saw the woman walking on the rails, and his hand moved towards the detonator-bag as though it was his intention to bring the speeding train to a halt. Fortunately it was too late, for already there was a flurry of lights before Thiel's eyes and the train tore past.

For the rest of the night Thiel found little peace any more in his duties. He felt an urge to be home. He longed to see young Tobias again. He had the feeling that he had been separated from him for years. Finally, in growing concern for the well-being of the boy, he was several times tempted to leave his post.

In order to pass the time, Thiel resolved to inspect his section of the track. Carrying a stick in his left hand and in his right a long iron spanner, he accordingly set off into the dirty grey half-light, walking along the top of one of the rails.

From time to time he tightened a bolt with the spanner or banged one of the round iron bars that bound the tracks together.

Rain and wind had abated, and here and there between rents in the cloudbanks patches of pale blue sky became visible.

The uniform clatter of his soles on the hard metal, combined with the sleepy sound of the dripping trees, gradually calmed Thiel.

At six a.m. he was relieved and instantly set off for home.

It was a glorious Sunday morning.

The clouds had broken up and sunk from view behind the wide circle of the horizon. The sun, sparkling as it rose like an enormous blood-red jewel, poured veritable masses of light over the forest.

Massed shafts of light pierced the tangle of trunks in

73

sharp lines, here breathing warmth into an island of tender ferns whose fronds were like delicately worked lace, there transforming the silver-grey lichens of the forest floor into red coral.

From tree-tops, trunks and grasses the fiery dew ran. A cleansing flood of light seemed to be poured over the earth. There was a freshness in the air that penetrated to the heart, and even behind Thiel's brow the images of the night gradually became fainter.

From the moment, however, when he entered his room and saw Tobias lying in the sun-bathed bed more red-cheeked than ever, they were completely gone.

It certainly seemed so. In the course of the day Lena several times thought she perceived something strange about him; in the pew at church, for instance, when, instead of looking at his book, he studied her from the side, and then at mid-day too when, without a word, he took the baby, whom Tobias was as usual due to carry into the street, from his arm and placed it on her lap. Otherwise, however, there was nothing in the least strange about him.

Thiel, who in the course of the day had not managed to get a rest, crept into bed as early as nine o'clock in the evening, since he was on daytime duty in the week that followed. Just as he was about to fall asleep his wife informed him that she would go with him the next morning to the woods, to dig over the land and plant potatoes.

Thiel started violently; he was fully awake again, but kept his eyes shut tight.

It was high time, said Lena, if the potatoes were to come to anything, and added that she would have to take the children along, as the task would probably occupy the whole day. The lineman muttered some unintelligible words, to which Lena paid no further attention. She had turned her back to him and was busy in the candlelight unlacing her bodice and letting down her skirts.

Suddenly she turned about, without herself knowing why, and looked into the ashen face of her husband, distorted by passion as he stared at her with burning eyes, half-upright, his hands on the edge of the bed.

'Thiel!' cried his wife, half in anger, half in fright, and like a sleepwalker who has been called by name he awoke from his stupefaction, stuttered a few jumbled words, threw himself back on the pillows and pulled the quilt over his ears.

Lena was the first out of bed the following morning. Without making any noise in the process, she got everything ready for the outing. The younger child was placed in his perambulator and then Tobias was wakened and dressed. When he learned where they were going he couldn't help smiling. When everything had been prepared and even the coffee was ready on the table Thiel woke up. Displeasure was his first feeling at the sight of all the preparations that had been made. He would have liked to say a word in protest, but he didn't know how to begin. And what reasons could he have given that would be valid for Lena?

Then gradually the increasingly radiant little face began to exert its influence on Thiel, so that in the end, if only for the sake of the joy which the outing was bringing the boy, he could not think of raising objections. Nevertheless, Thiel was not free from a feeling of unease during their walk through the woods. He pushed the perambulator laboriously through the deep sand, and soon all sorts of flowers were lying on it, gathered by Tobias.

The boy was unusually merry. He hopped about in his little brown velvet cap among the ferns and bracken and made clumsy attempts to catch the glaze-winged dragonflies which hovered over them. As soon as they arrived, Lena surveyed the plot of land. She threw the small sack of potato segments, which she had brought for planting, on the grass verge of a little birch copse, knelt down and let the dark-coloured sand run through her hard fingers.

Thiel watched her intently: 'Well, what's it like?'

'Every bit as good as the land by the Spree!' A weight fell from the lineman's heart. He had been afraid she would be dissatisfied, and scratched the stubble of his beard in relief.

After his wife had hastily devoured a thick chunk of bread, she threw off scarf and jacket and began to dig with the speed and tenacity of a machine.

At set intervals she straightened herself and took in deep breaths of air, but each time it was only for a moment, unless the baby needed to be fed, which was rapidly carried out at a breast that heaved and dripped with sweat.

'I must patrol the section, I'll take Tobias with me,' the lineman shouted over to her after a while from the platform in front of his hut.

'What's that – nonsense!' she shouted back, 'who's going to stay with the baby? – Come over here!' she continued still louder, while the lineman, as though unable to hear her, set off with young Tobias.

For a moment she considered whether she should run after them, and only the thought of the waste of time made her decide against this. Thiel went along the track with Tobias. The youngster was not a little excited; everything was new and strange to him. He did not understand the meaning of the narrow black rails warmed by the sunlight. Incessantly he asked all kinds of strange questions. The oddest thing of all for him was the singing of the telegraph poles. Thiel knew the sound of every single one on his beat, so that he would always have known with his eyes closed in which part of the section he happened to be.

Frequently he stopped, holding young Tobias by the hand, to listen to the wonderful sounds that issued from the posts like sonorous chorales surging forth from the interior of a church. The pole at the southern end of the stretch had a particularly full and beautiful harmony. There was a tumult of sounds within it, which flowed without interruption as though in one long breath, and Tobias ran around the weather-beaten timber thinking he could discover through an opening what was causing these delightful sounds. A mood of solemnity came over the lineman, as in church. And presently he was able to distinguish a voice which reminded him of his dead wife. He imagined to himself that it was a choir of blessed spirits, to which she also added her voice, and this thought wakened in him a longing that brought him to the point of tears.

Tobias hankered after the flowers that grew further back from the track, and Thiel, as always, gave in to him.

Pieces of blue sky seemed to have settled on the floor of the wood, so wonderfully close together did small blue flowers stand there. Like little coloured pennants, butterflies fluttered and tumbled silently between the gleaming white of the birch trunks, while a gentle rustling went through the tender green leaf-masses of the treetops.

Tobias gathered flowers, and his father watched him thoughtfully, from time to time also looking up; through the gaps in the leaves his eyes sought the sky, which gathered the golden light of the sun like a gigantic, immaculately blue crystal bowl.

'Father, is that our dear Lord?' asked the boy suddenly, pointing to a brown squirrel which scurried up the trunk of an isolated pine with scratching noises.

'Crazy child,' was all that Thiel could reply, while torn-off pieces of bark from the trunk landed in front of his feet.

The mother was still digging when Thiel and Tobias returned. Half of the plot had already been turned over.

The trains followed one another at short intervals, and each time Tobias watched them open-mouthed as they tore past.

Even the mother was amused by his droll expressions.

The mid-day meal, consisting of potatoes and the remainder of a cold roast of pork, was eaten in the hut. Lena was in a good mood, and even Thiel seemed to be accepting the inevitable with a good grace. He entertained his wife during the meal with all sorts of matters connected with his job. Thus he asked her if she could imagine that in one single length of rail there were forty-six screws, and similar things.

By the end of the morning Lena had finished digging over the land: in the afternoon the potatoes were to be planted out. She insisted that Tobias must now look after the baby, and took him with her.

'Watch out . . .' Thiel shouted after her, suddenly seized with concern. 'Watch out that he doesn't go too near the rails.'

A shrugging of the shoulders was Lena's answer.

The Silesian express was signalled and Thiel had to go to his post. Scarcely was he standing ready for duty at the barrier than he heard it roaring towards him.

The train hove into sight – it came nearer – in innumerable rapidly successive bursts it spat steam from its black funnel. Then: one – two – three milk-white columns of steam rose vertically upwards and immediately afterwards the engine's whistle was borne on the air. Three times in succession, short, shrill, alarming. They're braking, thought Thiel, but why? And once again the danger whistle shrilled stridently, waking the echoes, this time in a long unbroken sequence.

Thiel stepped forward, to be able to survey the track. Mechanically he drew his red flag out of its cover and held it straight in front of him over the lines. . . Jesus Christ – had he been blind? Jesus Christ – O, Jesus, Jesus, Jesus Christ! What was that? There! – there between the rails . . . 'Halt!' cried the lineman with all his might. Too late. A dark mass had gone under the train and was being tossed about between the wheels like a rubber ball. A few moments more, and the jarring and squealing of the brakes was heard. The train had stopped.

The lonely stretch of track came alive. Driver and guard ran along the chippings to the end of the train. From every window curious faces looked out and now – the crowd gathered and came forward.

Thiel gasped; he had to hold himself firm, so as not to sink to the ground like a felled ox. They are actually beckoning to him – 'No!'

A shriek rends the air from the scene of the accident, a howling follows, as though from the throat of an animal. Who was that? Lena?! It was not her voice, and yet . . .

A man comes hurrying up the track.

'Lineman!'

'What is it?'

'An accident!' . . . The messenger shrinks back, for the lineman's eyes glint strangely. His cap sits awry, his red hair seems to rear up.

'He's still alive, perhaps we can still save him.'

A choking sound is the only reply.

'Come on, quick, quick!'

Thiel pulls himself together with a mighty effort. His limp muscles grow tense; he draws himself up to his full height, his face is blank and lifeless.

He runs with the messenger, he does not see the deathly pale, shocked faces of the passengers at the carriage windows. A young woman looks out, a commercial representative in a fez, a young couple apparently on their honeymoon journey. What does it matter to him? He has never concerned himself with the contents of these upholstered boxes – his ear is filled with Lena's howling. Everything swims confusedly before his eyes, yellow dots, like glow-worms, in countless numbers. He shrinks back – stands still. Out of the dance of the glow-worms it emerges, pale, limp, bleeding. A forehead, battered black and blue, blue lips, over which black blood trickles. It's him.

Thiel does not speak. His face takes on a dirty pallor. He smiles absently: at last he bends down; he feels the limp, dead limbs heavy in his arms; the red flag wraps itself round them.

He goes off.

But where?

'To the district doctor, the district doctor,' everyone cries.

'We'll take him with us straight away,' shouts the luggage-master, and makes up a bed of uniforms and books in his van. 'How about that?'

Thiel shows no readiness to surrender the injured child. They argue with him. In vain. The luggage-master has a stretcher passed down from the luggage van and orders a man to assist the father.

Time is precious. The whistle of the engine-driver shrills. Coins rain from the windows.

Lena behaves as though demented. 'The poor, poor woman,' people say in the carriages, 'the poor, poor mother.'

The driver whistles again – a hoot – the engine ejects white, hissing steam from its cylinders and stretches its iron sinews; a few seconds more and the courier express will be roaring at double speed through the forest with its smoke trailing behind it.

The lineman, changing his mind, lays the half-dead boy on the stretcher. There he lies now, in his misshapen form, and from time to time a long, rattling gasp swells his bony chest, which comes into view under the tattered shirt. The tiny arms and legs, broken not only at the joints, assume the most unnatural postures. The heel of his little foot faces forward. His arms trail over the side of the stretcher.

Lena whimpers incessantly; every trace of her former defiance has gone from her being. She repeats constantly a story that exonerates her from all blame.

Thiel does not seem to heed her; his eyes are fixed in

ghastly fear on the child.

It has become still in the vicinity, deadly still; black and hot the rails lie on the dazzling chippings. The mid-day hour has stifled the winds, and the forest stands motionless, as if of stone.

The men deliberate quietly. To get to Friedrichshagen the quickest way they must go back to the station in the Breslau direction, as the next train, a limited stop local train, does not stop at the one nearer Friedrichshagen.

Thiel seems to consider whether he should go with them. At the moment there is nobody who can take over his duties. A mute gesture of the hand tells his wife to take up the stretcher; she does not dare resist, although she is concerned about the infant she is leaving behind. She and the stranger carry the stretcher. Thiel accompanies the train to the boundary of his territory, then he stands and gazes after it for a long time. Suddenly he strikes his forehead with the flat of his hand, sending an echo far around him.

He believes he is waking himself up, 'for it will be a dream, like the one yesterday,' he tells himself.

In vain.

More staggering than running he reached his hut. Inside he fell to the ground; face foremost. His cap rolled into the corner, his carefully tended watch fell from his pocket, the case flew open, the glass shattered. It was as if an iron fist had him by the neck, so tightly that he could not move, however much he tried, groaning and moaning, to free himself. His brow was cold, his eyes dry, his throat burned.

The alarm bell woke him. Under the impact of those repeated threefold bursts of the bell the attack subsided. Thiel could rise and do his duty. His feet were heavy as lead, the track spun around him like a spoke of an enormous wheel, whose axle was his head; but he at least gained enough strength to hold himself upright for a short while.

The local train approached. Tobias must be on it. The closer it came, the more blurred the images grew before Thiel's eyes. Finally he saw only the battered child with the bloody mouth. Then it was night.

After a while he awoke from his stupor. He found himself lying close by the barrier in the hot sand. He stood up, shook the grains of sand from his clothing and spat them from his mouth. His head was becoming a little clearer, he could think more calmly.

Inside the hut he immediately picked up his watch from the floor and laid it on the table. In spite of its fall it had not stopped. For two whole hours he counted the seconds and minutes, while imagining to himself what might be happening to Tobias in the meantime. Now Lena was arriving with him; now she was standing in front of the doctor. He studied and felt the boy and shook his head.

'Bad, very bad – but perhaps . . . who knows.' He made a closer examination. 'No,' he said then, 'no, it's hopeless.'

'Hopeless, hopeless,' groaned the lineman, then he drew himself up tall and shouted, his rolling eyes fixed on the ceiling, his raised hands unconsciously clenched into fists, and in a voice that seemed to burst the confined space asunder: 'He must, must live, I tell you, he must, must live.' And he flung the door of the hut open again, letting in the red fire of evening, and ran rather than walked back to the barrier. Here he stood for a while, as though confounded, and then stepped suddenly into the middle of the track, both arms extended, as though seeking to stop something that was coming from the direction taken by the local train. As he did so his wide-open eyes gave the impression of blindness.

Stepping backwards, he appeared to be giving way to something, and half-intelligible words issued continuously from between his teeth: 'Do you hear me – stop – listen – stop – give him back – he's beaten black and blue – yes, yes – all right, I'll beat *her* black and blue – do you hear? Oh do stop – give him back to me.'

It seemed as though something went past him, for he turned and moved in the opposite direction, as though to pursue it.

'Minna' – his voice became whining, like that of a small child. 'Minna, do you hear? – Give him back – I want . . .' He groped in the air, as though to hold someone tight. 'My dear – yes – and then I'll – then I'll beat her as well – black and blue – beat her – and I'll take the axe – do you hear? – the kitchen axe – I'll hit her, with the kitchen axe, and she'll die like a dog.

'And then . . . yes, with the axe – the kitchen axe, yes – black blood!' Froth covered his mouth, his glazed pupils were in constant motion.

A gentle evening breeze stirred the forest, quietly and steadily, and soft tresses of cloud shot with pink hung over the western sky.

He had followed the invisible something in this way for about a hundred paces when he stopped still, seeming to lose hope, and with a dreadful anguish in his features the man stretched out his arms, appealing, beseeching. He strained his eyes and shaded them with his hand, as if once more to discern an insubstantial being in the far distance. Finally his hand sank, and the tensed expression on his face changed to a blank inexpressiveness; he turned and trailed back the way he had come.

The sun poured its last glow over the forest, and then was extinguished. The trunks of the pines thrust up like pale, decayed bones among the tree-tops, which rested upon them like greyish-black layers of mould. The hammering of a woodpecker rang out through the stillness. Across the cold, steel-blue spaces of the sky there drifted an isolated late wisp of pink cloud. The wind's breath became cold as a cellar, so that the lineman shivered. Everything was new to him, everything strange. He did not know what he was walking upon or what was around him. Then a squirrel darted across the track and Thiel mused to himself. He couldn't help thinking of the dear Lord, without knowing why. 'The dear Lord is running across the track, the dear Lord is running across the track.' He repeated the sentence several times, as though seeking to hit upon something that was connected with it. He broke off, a glimmer of light flashed into his brain: 'My God, but that's madness.' He forgot everything and turned to face this new enemy. He sought to bring his thoughts into order, but in vain. There was no holding their rambling and roaming. He caught himself out in the most absurd imaginings and shuddered in the consciousness of his helplessness.

From the nearby birchwood came the crying of a child. It was the signal for all control to break down. Almost against his will he had to hurry to it and found the infant, whom nobody had bothered about, crying and kicking in its pram without bedding. What was his intention? What drove him here? A whirl of thoughts and feelings engulfed these questions.

'The dear Lord is running across the track,' now he knew what it meant. 'Tobias' – she had murdered him – Lena – he was in her care – 'Stepmother, false mother,' he gritted, 'and her own brat lives.' A red mist enveloped his senses, pierced by a child's eyes; he felt something soft, fleshy between his fingers. Sounds of gurgling and wheezing interspersed with hoarse shouts – he didn't know who they came from – struck his ear.

Then something fell into his brain like drops of hot sealing-wax, and his mind was released as if from a cramp. Coming to consciousness, he heard the echo of the signal bell vibrating through the air.

In a flash he understood what his intention had been: his hand loosened on the throat of the child, which was writhing in his grip. It fought for air, then it began to cough and cry.

'It's alive. Thank God, it's alive!' He left it lying and hurried to the crossing. Dark smoke curled about over the track in the distance and the wind drove it to the ground. Behind him he heard the wheezing of an engine, which sounded like the fitfully agonised breathing of a sick giant.

A cold twilight lay over the region.

After a while, when the smoke-clouds cleared away, Thiel recognised the gravel train, which was returning with emptied trucks, taking with it the labourers who had been working during the day on the track.

The train had a liberally defined time-schedule and was permitted to stop anywhere to pick up the labourers who were working at various points and to set others down. A good distance before Thiel's hut the train began to brake. A loud squeaking, clanking, rattling and clattering penetrated deep into the calm of evening, until the train came to a stop with one single shrill, drawn-out noise.

About fifty workers, men and women, were distributed about the trucks. Almost all of them stood erect, some of the men with bared heads. In the manner of all lay an enigmatic solemnity. When they caught sight of the lineman, a whispering started amongst them. The old men took their pipes from between their yellow teeth and held them respectfully in their hands. Here and there a woman turned to blow her nose. The engine-driver climbed down onto the track and went up to Thiel. The workers saw him solemnly shake his hand, after which Thiel walked with slow, almost militarily stiff gait to the last waggon.

None of the workers dared to address him, although they all knew him.

From the last waggon they were just lifting little Tobias.

He was dead.

Lena followed him: her face was a bluish-white, brown circles lay around her eyes.

Thiel did not so much as look at her; but she was alarmed by the appearance of her husband. His cheeks were hollow, the eyelashes and beard matted, his head, it seemed to her, greyer than before. Traces of dried-up tears everywhere on his face, and in addition a shifting light in his eyes, which caused her to shudder.

The stretcher had also been brought along again, in order to transport the body.

For a while an uncanny stillness reigned. A profound, terrible introspection had taken hold of Thiel. It was becoming darker. A small herd of deer took to the track a little further off. The stag stopped right in the centre of the rails. He turned his supple neck inquisitively, at that moment the engine whistled, and in a flash he disappeared together with his herd.

At the moment when the train was about to move off, Thiel collapsed.

The train stopped again and a consultation ensued about what was to be done now. They decided to place the body of the child for the time being in the lineman's hut, and in its stead to take home the lineman, whom no means proved capable of recalling to consciousness, by means of the bier.

And this was done. Two men carried the stretcher bearing the unconscious man, followed by Lena, who, continuously sobbing and with tear-drenched face, pushed the perambulator with the youngster through the sand.

Like a giant sphere, glowing purple, the moon sat between the shafts of the pines on the floor of the forest. The higher it climbed the smaller it seemed to grow, the paler it became. At last it hung lamp-like over the forest, filtering through all crevices and gaps in the tree-tops with a thin luminosity which imparted a corpse-like quality to the faces of the walkers.

Sturdily, yet carefully, they strode on, now through close-set young timber, now over broad clearings ringed with mature forest, in which the pale light had gathered as though in huge, dark basins.

The unconscious man gave a throaty rattle from time to time or began to ramble. Several times he clenched his fists and attempted to sit up with eyes closed.

They had considerable trouble in getting him over the Spree; they had to make the crossing a second time to fetch the wife and child.

As they climbed the small rise into the village, they met some of the inhabitants, who immediately spread the news of the accident that had occurred.

The entire settlement came out onto the street.

At the sight of her neighbours, Lena broke into fresh lamentations.

The sick man was conveyed, with much difficulty, up the narrow steps of his house and put to bed immediately. The workers set off again instantly to fetch Tobias's body.

Old people, with experience, advised cold compresses, and Lena followed their directions with diligence and care. She put towels into ice-cold well-water and renewed them as soon as the burning brow of the unconscious man had dried them through. Anxiously she watched the breathing of the sick man, which seemed to her to become more regular each minute.

The day's exertions had however told on her severely, and she decided to sleep a little, but found no rest. Whether she opened her eyes or closed them, the events that had taken place constantly appeared before her. The baby slept; contrary to her usual custom, she had concerned herself very little with him. She had become an entirely different person. No trace of the old truculence. Indeed, this sick man with the colourless, sweat-glistening face ruled her in his sleep.

A cloud hid the moon's circle, it became dark in the room, and Lena heard only the heavy but regular breathing of her husband. She considered whether she should light a lamp. She felt uneasy in the dark. When she tried to stand up, her limbs were like lead, her eyelids closed, she fell asleep.

After the passing of some hours, when the men came back with the child's body, they found the door of the house wide open. Puzzled by this circumstance they climbed the stairs to the upper part of the house, where the door was likewise wide open.

They called the wife's name several times, without receiving a reply. Finally they struck a match on the wall, and as the light flared up it revealed a scene of gruesome devastation.

'Murder! Murder!'

Lena lay in her blood, her face unrecognisable, her skull shattered.

'He's murdered his wife, he's murdered his wife!'

They ran about in confusion. The neighbours came, one of them knocked against the cradle. 'Oh God Almighty!' And he started back, white-faced, his eyes stark with horror. The child lay with his throat cut.

The lineman had disappeared; the searches which were organised that very same night were without result. The following morning the lineman on duty found him sitting between the railway lines at the point where Tobias had been run over.

He was holding the little brown velvet cap in his arm and stroking it constantly like something living.

The railwayman addressed some questions to him but received no reply and soon realised that he was dealing with someone out of his mind.

The railman in the signal-box, informed of this, requested help via the telegraph.

Several men now attempted to entice him away from the lines by friendly persuasion; but in vain.

The express which went through at this time had to stop, and it was only the superior strength of its crew that was successful in removing the ailing man, who had immediately become terribly violent, forcibly from the track.

They had to tie his hands and feet, and the policeman who had meanwhile been sent for supervised his transportation to the investigation detention centre in Berlin, from where he was however conveyed on the very first day to an insane ward. On admission he still held the little brown cap in his hands, guarding it with jealous care and affection.

The Apostle

He had reached Zurich late in the evening. An attic room in the 'Dove', a little bread and clear water before he laid himself to rest: that sufficed.

He slept restlessly for only a few hours. Shortly after four he had already risen. His head pained him. He put it down to the long railway journey of the previous day. To endure something like that you had to have nerves like steel. He hated these railways with their eternal rattling, pounding and banging, with their fleeting images – he hated them and together with them most of the other so-called attainments of this so-called culture.

The Gotthard alone . . . it really was a torture travelling through the Gotthard:* sitting there by the light of a little flickering lamp, aware of having that enormous mass of stone above you. And then that concert of noises in your ear, shattering every fibre in your body. It was a torture to drive you insane! He had got into a state, into a degree of anxiety that was scarcely credible. When the roaring close at hand receded and then approached again, raging like all hell itself, and became such a clamour that it shattered everything

* The St. Gotthard rail tunnel, 9½ miles in length, was opened in 1882. One of the greatest engineering feats of the nineteenth century, it supplanted the transalpine road from Lucerne to Milan that had been in use since the thirteenth century.

inside you to fragments . . . never, never again would he travel through the Gotthard!

You only had one head. Once it was stirred up – the swarm of bees that nestled in there – then the devil himself would be hard put to restore calm again; everything burst its bounds, lost its natural proportions, reared up and had a will of its own.

During the night it had still tormented him, now it was to come to an end. The cold, clear morning must play its part. From here on, he would travel into Germany on foot.

He washed and pulled on his clothes. As he fastened on his sandals, he had a fleeting glimpse of how he had come by the garb that he now wore and that distinguished him from all other people: the figure of Master Dieffenbach crossed his vision. Then came a leap back into childhood years: he saw himself going to school in so-called normal clothes – the bald head of his father looked out from behind the counter of the chemist's shop, mildly ridiculing his son's dress. But his mother had always maintained that he was not a depressive type. The bald pate and the young womanly face drew close together. What a colossal difference! Strange that he had never noticed it before.

His sandals were firmly fastened. He placed the cord that held the white baize habit together about his hips and tied a braid around his head.

In the entrance hall of the inn an old mirror had been fixed. As he passed by he paused for a moment to inspect himself. He really looked like an apostle! The saintly blond of his long hair, the strong red wedge-shaped beard, the bold, firm and yet infinitely gentle face, the white monk's robe, which showed to perfection his fine, upright figure and supple, militarily schooled body.

He gazed with satisfaction at his reflection. Why indeed should he not? Why should he not admire his own self, since he never ceased to wonder at Nature in all that she brought forth? His course through the world took him from wonder to wonder, and objects that others ignored called forth in him feelings of sacred delight. Incidentally, it made a good impression, the innovation of this morning: it could well be believed that this band around his head had the purpose of gathering his hair. The fact that it resembled a halo was of no significance. There were no saints any longer, or rather – every single product of Nature, even the tiniest of little flowers or beetles, had its halo, and it was a profane eye indeed that saw no such haloes hovering over all things.

On the street nobody was yet about: solitary sunshine lay upon it; here and there the long, rather oblique shadow of a house. He turned into a side alley which rose with the slope of the hill and was soon climbing upwards between meadows and orchards.

From time to time a high-gabled, old-style cottage, the little narrow garden of a house full to the brim with flowers, then again a meadow or a vineyard. The scent of white jasmine, blue lilac and dark-glowing wallflowers filled the clear, strong air in places, so that he imbibed it contentedly like a spiced wine.

He felt freer with every step.

It was as though a thorn were loosening itself from his heart, as his eye was drawn so quietly and irresistibly outwards. The darkness within him was consumed by all the light. The heads of the yellow dandelions, laid like innumerable little suns into the sprouting green of the wayside, almost blinded him. Through the heavy rain of blossom from the fruit trees the sun's rays shot obliquely into the meadow-filled valley, covering it with golden flecks. The birches smelt so honey-sweet. And so much life, contentment and vigour spoke from the vain humming of early bees.

As he climbed he carefully avoided damaging or destroying anything living. The tiniest beetle was circumvented, the importunate wasp carefully chased away. He loved the midges and flies as brothers, and to kill – even if it were only the most commonplace cabbage-white – seemed to him the worst of all crimes.

Flowers, half-faded, plucked by children's hands, he gathered up from the path, to throw them into water somewhere. He himself never picked violets or roses for self-adornment. He abominated bouquets and wreaths: he wished everything to be in its rightful place.

He felt well and contented. His only regret was that he could not see himself. Himself with his noble gait, climbing alone in the early morning up into the mountains: that would have provided a motif for a great painter; and the picture stood before him in his imagination.

Then he looked around to see if perhaps some human soul was already awake and could see him. Nobody was in sight.

Now the strange chattering – in his ear or even inside his head, he didn't know where – started up again. For some weeks it had been plaguing him. It was congestion of the blood, to be sure. You had to run, exert yourself, bring the blood into faster circulation.

And he speeded up his steps.

He had thus gradually emerged above the roofs of the houses. He stood still, resting, and had all the splendour of the scene beneath him. He experienced a shock. A feeling of profound remorse burned within him at the wonderful prospect below. For a long time he allowed his enraptured eye to luxuriate in the splendour around him – away above it all, up to the peak of the mountain opposite, whose creviced slopes were clad in gentle, woollen green; downwards where the violet-hued surface of the lake filled the valley bottom, whence the soft, grassy hills that enclosed it climbed away upwards, green pillows inundated as far as the eye could reach with blossom upon blossom. In between, cottages, villas and villages, their windows flashing with an electric vibrance, their red roofs and their towers gleaming.

Only to the south, far away, a silvery grey haze joined lake and sky and veiled the landscape; but above it, gleaming fine and white, set against the pale blue of the sky, they rose up in shadowy outline – like some gigantic hoard of silver – in a long, vanishing line: the tips of the snow-peaks.

There his gaze fastened, rigidly fixed, for a long time. When he was finally released, nothing firm was left in him. Everything soft, dissolved. Tears and sobs.

He moved on.

From above, where the beeches began, the call of the cuckoo met his ear: those two notes that are repeated, cease, and then begin again and again. He went on, now engrossed in himself, introspective.

Mysterious emotions when confronted with Nature were nothing unusual for him; but never before had they overcome him so strongly and abruptly as now. It was his feeling for Nature, which was becoming stronger and deeper. Nothing was more understandable, and there was no need to form hypochondriac thoughts about it.

Besides, things were starting to condense in him, to take firm shape, to assume form. It was scarcely a matter of minutes before everything in him was connected and firm.

He stood still, gazing once more. Now it was the town below that attracted and repelled him. It seemed to him like a grey, loathsome scab, like a scurf implanted into this paradise that would eat its way further: pile upon pile of stones, with sparse green inbetween. He grasped that man was the most dangerous vermin of all. Yes indeed, that was beyond all doubt: towns were no better than tumours, excrescences of culture. Their aspect caused him nausea and pain.

Reaching the beeches he sank down. Stretched out at full-length, his head close to the earth, inhaling the smell of humus and grass, the transparent green stems close before his eyes, he lay there. He was so filled with a sense of contentment, a swelling love, an ecstatic bliss. Like silver columns, the beech-trunks. Above them the surging, rustling green sungold-shot baldaquin, the singing, the joy, the fervent laughing jubilation of the birds. He closed his eyes and surrendered himself totally.

As he did so, the previous night's dream began to return to him: an unaccustomed mood at first, a beating of the heart, a sense of elevation that brought with it an impression over whose origins he was forced to reflect. At last the recollection came. Between day and evening. An unending, dusty Italian highway, still hot from the sun, radiating flickering heat. Country folk coming from the fields, brown, motley-coloured, ragged. Men, women and children with dark, piercing eyes, sick with faith. Wretched huts on the slopes. Ringing out over them the simple Catholic clamour of evening bells. He himself dusty, tired, hungry and thirsty. He strides on slowly, the people kneel by the wayside, they fold their hands, they worship him. He feels tenderness, he feels greatness.

He lay clinging to the image. Feverishness, desire, shudders of divine sublimity surged within him. He rose up like God.

Now as he opened his eyes, he was alarmed. Like a column of water it broke apart and dispersed.

Questioning and challenging himself he pressed into the midst of the wood. He reproached himself over his ecstatic dreaming: it happened against his wish and resolution. The very might of his feelings made him uneasy, and yet – it could be that his nagging anxiety was groundless.

They really had venerated him, the Italians whose villages he had passed through on foot. They had come to have their children blessed by him. Why should he not give blessing, when other priests were allowed to bless? He too had something – he had more to communicate than they. There was a word, a single, wonderful jewel of a word: peace! In it lay what he brought, in it everything was contained – everything – everything.

The smell of blood lay upon the world. Flowing blood was the sign of conflict. He heard this conflict raging, incessantly, waking and sleeping. It was brothers together, sisters together, who were killing one another. He loved them all, he saw their raging and wrung his hands in pain and despair.

To speak with the voice of thunder was his burning desire. In the face of the raging battle you had to stand on a great boulder, visible to all, calling and signalling. To warn against the killing of brother and sister, to point out the way to peace, was a demand of conscience.

He knew this path. You entered it through a gate with the inscription: Nature.

Courage and fervour had gradually ousted the anxiety in his soul once more. He went he knew not where, preaching in the spirit and speaking in private to all peoples: You are guzzlers and drunkards! Like cannibals you display the corpses of animals on your tables. Desist from your gluttony! Desist from the ruthless slaughter of fellow-creatures! Let fruits of the field be your nourishment! Your silken beds, your cushions, your precious furniture and clothes, bring them all together, throw torches upon them, so that the flames reach up to Heaven and consume them! When you have done that, then come – come, all of you who are weary and burdened, and follow me! I will lead you to a land where tiger and buffalo graze together, where snakes are without venom and bees without sting. There the hatred within you will die and love eternal shall become alive.

His heart swelled. Like a raging stream the torrent of reproachful, comforting and admonishing words poured forth. His entire body trembled with passion. The urge to pour forth the whole of his love and longing overwhelmed him. He felt as though he must preach to the trees and the birds. The power of his speech must be irresistible. He could have laid a spell, with a single word, upon the squirrel that went scampering by in bounding leaps through the branches, and called it to him. He knew it, knew it for certain, as one knows that a stone will fall. An almighty power lay within him: the almighty power of truth.

Suddenly the wood came to an end. Almost frightened and blinded, like someone emerging from a deep shaft, he saw the world. But the tumult within him did not cease. Of a sudden, direction came into his steps. He descended, running and jumping on the steep path.

Like a soldier in the attack, his goal in view; thus he now seemed to himself. Once he had started to run, it was difficult to stop. The swift, violent movement roused something in him; a joyous feeling, a kind of excitement, a madness.

Consciousness returned and with horror he saw himself rushing down the hillside in great bounds. Something within him wanted to call a rapid halt, impose restraint, but it was already a sea that had burst the dams. A paralysing fear crouched in the depths of his soul and with it a horrified, nameless amazement.

His body meanwhile, like something foreign to him, tore on unshackled. He clapped his hands together, ground his teeth, and stamped on the ground. He laughed – laughed louder and louder, without a break.

When he came to himself he was trembling. Almost paralysed with horror, he was clinging to the trunk of a young lime. Only with great care and in the constant dread of a return of that unknown, fearful force, did he go on again. He did however become free and sure of himself once more, so that in the end he was able to smile at his state of anxiety.

Now, with the firm regularity of his steps and with the first houses in sight, there came the memory of his time as a soldier. How often, his heart filled to bursting with the silent exultation of vanity satisfied, had he as a lieutenant come marching in at the side of his platoon to the sound of music playing. Scarcely had he thought of it than the sturdy, fiery marching music had started up in his head, the sound that had so often roused fanatical emotions in him. It rang in his ear and caused him to walk in step and bare head and chest with unusual pride. It laid a victorious smile upon his lips and a lively gleam in his eyes. Marching along in this way, he listened at the same time to the sounds within him, amazed that he was able to distinguish so sharply every note, every chord, every instrument, right down to the reverberation of the clash of drum and cymbal. He did not know whether to be disturbed or pleased by the strength of his imagination. Without a doubt it was an aptitude. He had a musical aptitude He would certainly have created great compositions. How many aptitudes could well have been stifled within him? But that was unimportant. All art was nonsense, poison. There were other, more important things for him to do.

A girl in a blue calico dress, with a pink wrap, came towards him, a tin can in her hand: she was evidently delivering milk. He had glanced at her quickly and seen her stop in amazement at his appearance and look at him open-eyed. She then greeted him with respectful emphasis in a subdued voice, and he passed her by with moderated step and earnest acknowledgement.

At once all within him was silent. At that moment he far transcended his previous little fantasies. If he still bore something like music in his ear, then it was certainly no earthly melody. He strode on with the sensation of walking dry-footed over water. So sublime and great did he seem to himself that he admonished himself to humility. And as he did so, he could not help recalling Christ's entry into Jerusalem and in conclusion the words: 'Behold, thy King cometh unto thee, meek . . .'

For a time still he felt the gaze of the girl following him. For some reason, as he walked on, he kept as exactly as possible to the middle of the track, even when he turned into a broad white road with a downhill slope. As he did so, as though under some form of compulsion, he could not help repeating, again and again: 'Thy King cometh unto thee.'

Children's voices sang these words. They lay still unformed between his gums and tongue. From the unarticulated sound of his breathing he could hear their tones. Amongst them hosannas, rustling palm fronds, shouts of joy, pale, ecstatic faces. Then again, abrupt stillness – loneliness.

He looked up, filled with amazement. Everywhere like an empty stage. Stone houses to right and left, silent, austere, sleepy. Thoughtfully he checked it all. Gradually, as it was substantiated, his inner self began to adjust to it. And so he became small, simple and began to look about soberly.

Here and there a window stood open. The head of a servant-girl became visible, a bedside rug was being beaten. A student, dark-haired and with fleshy lips, apparently a Russian, rolled his breakfast cigarette on the window-ledge. And already the street was becoming more alive. His eyes fixed to the ground, he nevertheless did not neglect to look stealthily about him. Sometimes he looked straight into broad impudent laughter. Sometimes he noticed how amazement ruled out mockery. But behind his back the mockery then broke free, and bold expressions, sharp and biting, flew after him.

With every step taken amidst so many jibes and blows, he felt more banal. There was a tightness in his throat. The old, bitter, hopeless grief emerged. Like a wall, thick and unsurmountable, the cruel blindness of man rose up before him.

Now it suddenly seemed to him as though all denial

was useless. He was indeed after all only a vain, small, shallow being. He was only getting his deserts when people scorned and mocked him. Thus for several minutes on end he experienced the agony and shame of an unmasked confidence trickster and the desire to run away from everybody, to crawl into a corner, to hide himself, or in some way to put an end altogether to his life.

If he had been alone now, he would have torn off and burned the cord around his head that looked like a halo. As though wearing a fool's paper crown, half-destroyed by shame, he walked beneath it.

He had turned off into narrow, labyrinthine backstreets without sunshine. A small window full of baked wares drew him to it. He opened the glass door and entered the shop. The baker looked at him – the baker's wife – he selected a small loaf, said nothing and went.

Outside the door a crowd of curious people had gathered: an old woman, children, a butcher's assistant, his tray with pieces of red meat on his shoulder. He scanned their faces quickly, there was nothing impudent about them, and went his way through their midst.

With what expressions they had all looked at him! First of all the people in the bakery. As though he did not need the loaf for eating, but rather to perform a miracle with it. And why did people wait for him in front of their doors? There must be some reason. And now all that clatter of feet and whispering behind him. Why were people following him? Why was he being pursued?

He listened intently and soon became aware that he had a following of children behind him. By crossing this way and that over little squares with old fountains in them, turning deliberately about and changing direction, he made certain that the little group would not let him go.

Why were they pursuing him and wanting to see so much of him? Did they expect more from him? Did they actually hope to see something new, extraordinary, marvellous from him? It seemed as though from the monotonous haste in the sound of their feet there spoke a strong faith, indeed, more still than this: a conviction. And suddenly he saw quite clearly why prophets, genuine men of greatness and purity, so often in the end become common deceivers. He experienced suddenly a burning desire, an irresistible urge, to perform something wonderful, and the greatest disgrace would have appeared small to him in comparison with the admission of his ineffectuality.

He had in the meantime reached the quay beside the Limmat,* and still the youngsters followed him. Some ran, the bigger ones took inordinately long strides to keep up with him. Their conversation consisted in snatches of words, produced in the solemn whisper of church tradition. He had so far not been able to understand anything of what they said. Suddenly however – he had heard it quite clearly – the words 'Lord Jesus' were pronounced.

The effect of magic lay in these words. He felt himself elevated by them, fortified, restored.

Jesus had been mocked: they had beaten him, spat on him and nailed him to the Cross. Scorn and derision were the reward of all prophets. His own small sufferings did not come into consideration. Little, cowardly

---

* Which flows through Zurich and the Lake.

pinpricks had been inflicted on him. Only a weakling would be destroyed by them!

It was for conflict that one was here. Wounds gave proof of the warrior. Mockery and scorn from the crowd . . . what higher marks of distinction were to be gained? One's breast adorned with them, one could look proudly and freely on the world. And furthermore; out of the mouth of babes and sucklings hast thou ordained strength.

He came to a halt in front of a woman selling oranges. Immediately the youngsters also stopped running, and a crowd of inquisitive people built up on the pavement. He would dearly have liked to buy his fruit without speaking. The people waited in suspense for his first word, which made him embarrassed and shy. A confident feeling told him that he had an illusion to guard, that it depended on his mode of speaking whether his listeners would follow him further or slip away disillusioned. But it was not to be avoided, the huckster-woman questioned and chattered too much, and so in the end he had to speak.

He was relieved and satisfied as soon as he heard his own voice; there was a singing, dignified quality about it, a solemn and as it were melancholic gravity, which, he was convinced, was bound to make an effect. He had scarcely ever heard himself speak in this way, and while he spoke, the act itself gave him pleasure, like a singer with his song. On the bridge underneath which the blue-green lake sent its waves lapping, he stopped once more. Leaning over the balustrade, he drank in afresh the light, colour and freshness of the morning. The turbulent, invigorating wind, travelling up the lake, blew his beard over his shoulder and flowed about his forehead and chest like a cold bath.

And now, out of the spirited surging of his inner being, it rose as a firm resolve. The time had come. Something had to happen. Within him was a power to rouse mankind. Yes indeed! And however they might laugh, scorn and mock him, he would yet redeem them, all, all!

Now he began to meditate, sunk deep in thought. That it would come about was now firmly established; how it would come about had still to be considered. Today Whitsuntide was being celebrated, and that was good. At Whitsuntide the disciples of Jesus had spoken with tongues of fire. The mood of celebration meant receptiveness. The souls of men on holy days were like a prepared field.

Deeper and deeper he penetrated into his inner self, until he entered upon realms that were wide, high and infinite. And so completely sunk with all his senses into this second world was he that he walked on without conscious will, like a man asleep. Of all that surrounded him nothing penetrated any longer into his consciousness, apart from the patter of children's feet behind him.

Staying constant for a time, it gradually swelled in volume, as though the few who were following had been joined by others. And growing ever stronger, as if the few had become hundreds, the hundreds thousands.

Quite suddenly he became alert, and now it was as though, in his wake, whole armies were struggling.

Through his feet, as far as the ankles, he felt a trembling of the earth. He heard strong breathing behind him, hot, hurried whispers. He heard exultation, abruptly broken off, half-suppressed, which spread far to the rear and only died away in the far distance like an echo.

What that signified he knew full well. That it had come so amazingly quickly he had not anticipated. Through his limbs there burned the pride of a commander-in-chief, and the consciousness of an exceptional responsibility weighed no more heavily upon him than the cord on his head. He was after all the man that he was. He knew the way that he must lead them. He sensed from the laughing and urging of his soul that it was near to him, that final happiness of the world, for which blind humanity, with bleeding eyes and hands, had sought in vain for so many millennia.

So he strode on – he – he – yes, he! and into the imprint of his feet surged the people like waves of the sea. To him they looked up, the milliards. The last mocker had long since fallen silent. The last despiser had become a myth.

So he strode on, towards the mountains. Up there was the bourne behind which lay the land where happiness rested eternally in the arms of peace. And already happiness surged through him with a weight and a power which proved to him that one needed athletic muscles to endure it.

He had them, he had athletic muscles. His life, his whole existence was now merely a voluptuous, playful unfolding of strength.

He experienced a desire to play ball with rocks and trees. But behind him was the rustling of silken banners, and the ceaseless press and throb of the vast pilgrimage of humanity.

People shouted, people beckoned, people waved; black, blue, red veils fluttered; blond, unfastened women's hair; grey and white heads nodded; the flesh of bare, sinewy arms gleamed in the light; rapturous eyes, gazing to Heaven or turned fierily towards him, full of pure faith: towards him, striding onward.

And now he pronounced it, softly, scarcely audibly, the sacred jewel of a word – 'World-peace'! But it lived and flew back from one to the other. It was a murmured blend of emotion and solemnity. From afar came the wind and brought faint chords of incipient chorales. Muted trumpet sounds, human voices singing, hesitant and pure; until something broke like the ice of a river, and a hymn swelled up as from a thousand resounding organs. A hymn that was all soul and turbulence, and had an old melody that he knew: 'Now thank we all our God'.

He came to himself. His heart was pounding. He was close to weeping. Before his eyes white dots floated in confusion. His limbs were as though shattered.

He sat down on a bench at the edge of the lake and began to eat the bread that he had bought. Then he peeled the orange and pressed the cold peel to his brow. Reverently, like Christ the Host, he consumed the fruit. He had not yet finished it when he sank wearily back. A little sleep would have been welcome. Yes, if it had been so easy; to rest. How is rest to come when everything in one's head is in ceaseless uproar and ferment? When the heart yearns, when one is drawn into the Indeterminate – when one has a mission that requires one to submit to it – when humanity without is waiting and racked with uncertainty? How can one rest when there is a need for action?

It was an agonising condition as he lay there. Question upon question and never an answer. Grey, tormenting emptiness, from time to time painful pauses. He could not help thinking of a draw-well. Standing there, pulling with all your might on the rope, but the wheel over which it passes does not turn. Ceaselessly heaving and tugging. The bucket must come up. You are dying of thirst. The wheel does not yield. The rope will move neither forwards nor backwards . . . It was a torture, an ordeal – almost a physical suffering. When he heard steps he was glad of the diversion. Dear God! What sort of idea had that been, wanting to sleep now! He stood up, puzzled to find himself in his room, and opened the door to the hall. His mother, he knew, was standing in the passage and he had to let her in. She entered, looked at him with radiant admiration, her lips trembled and she folded her hands in reverence. He laid his hands on her head and said: 'Rise' – and – the sick woman rose and was able to walk. And as she stood up he saw that it was not his mother, but he, the sufferer from Nazareth. Not only had he healed him; he had returned him to life. The burial shroud still wafted about the body of Jesus. He came towards him and entered into him. And an ineffable music sounded as he thus entered into him. He experienced precisely the whole, sacred process, as the figure of Jesus dissolved into his own. He now saw the disciples who were seeking the Master. From among them Peter approached him and said: 'Rabbi!' – 'I am that man,' was his reply. And Peter came nearer, very close, touched his eyeball and began to turn it: the disciple was turning the globe. The hour had come to show himself to the people. Onto the balcony of the room in which he dwelled he stepped out. Below, the crowd surged, and into the ferment and surging the single, thin voice of a child sang: 'Christ is risen.'

It had scarcely begun to be heard when the ironwork of the balcony gave way. He received a violent fright, woke up, rubbed his eyes, and became aware that he had fallen asleep on the bench.

It must have been about mid-day. He wanted to go up into the beechwood again, to await his time. The sun would consecrate him, up there.

The air still cool and pure as he climbed the mountain. The hymns of birds. The sky like a pale blue, empty crystal bowl. Everything so immaculate. Everything so new.

He himself was new also. He studied his hand, it was the hand of a god; and how free and pure was his spirit! And this emancipation of the limbs, this total inner certainty and freedom from scruple. Speculation and thought were now at the furthest remove from his mind. He smiled full of pity when his thoughts travelled back to the philosophers of this world. That they thought they could establish something with their speculation was as touching as, say, the sight of a child struggling to fly into the air with his two bare little arms.

No, no – wings are required for that, the broad, giant pinions of an eagle – the power of a god!

He bore something like an enormous diamond in his head, whose light made bright all black depths and abysses: there was darkness no longer in his realm . . . The great knowledge had dawned.

The church-bells were beginning to peal. A turmoil and tumult of sounds filled the valley. The air seemed to speak with a tongue of brass.

He bent forward and listened as it ascended to him. He did not bow his head, he did not kneel. He listened with a smile as though to an old friend's voice, though it was God the Father who was speaking with his Son.

Also published by Angel Books

FICTION

ALFRED DÖBLIN
A People Betrayed *and* Karl and Rosa
(*The trilogy* November 1918: A German Revolution
complete in 2 volumes)
Translated by John E. Woods
0 88064 008 1 *and* 0 88064 011 1 (*paperback*)
*Published in the USA by Fromm International Publishing
Corporation, New York*

HEINRICH VON KLEIST/LUDWIG TIECK/E.T.A. HOFFMANN
Six German Romantic Tales
Translated by Ronald Taylor
0 946162 17 4 (*paperback*)

ADALBERT STIFTER
Brigitta
with Limestone, Abdias *and* The Forest Path
Translated by Helen Watanabe
0 946162 36 0 (*cased*)   0 946162 37 9 (*paperback*)

POETRY

JOHANN WOLFGANG VON GOETHE
Torquato Tasso
Translated by Alan Brownjohn with Sandy Brownjohn
Introduction by T.J. Reed
0 946162 19 0 (*paperback*)

HEINRICH HEINE
Deutschland
Translated by T.J. Reed
0 946162 21 2 (*cased*)   0 946162 22 0 (*paperback*)